Reena Spaulings

BERNADETTE CORPORATION

Reena Spaulings

Semiotext(e)

Credits

SEMIOTEXT(E) NATIVE AGENTS SERIES

Published by Semiotext(e)
P.O. Box 629, South Pasadena, CA 91031

Dieses Buch erscheint anlässlich der Ausstellung *Jetzt und zehn Jahre davor*, realisiert aus Mitteln des Hauptstadtkulturfonds Berlin 2004.

This book was published on the occasion of the exhibition *Now and Ten Years Ago*, funded through the Hauptstadtkulturfonds Berlin, 2004.

Additional funding provided by Toasting Agency, Paris.

Designed at The Royal Academy of Nuts + Bolts, D.O.D.,
in collaboration with Bernadette Corporation
www.TheRoyalAcademy.org
Cover art by Bernadette Corporation

ISBN: 978-1-58435-030-9
Distributed by the MIT Press
Printed and bound in the United States of America
10 9 8 7 6

Contents

Preface
Reena Spaulings

Preface

If you look at a city, there's no way to see it. One person can never see a city. You can miss it, hate it, or realize that it's taken something from you, but you can't go somewhere and look at it and just see it empirically. It has to be informed, imagined, by many people at a time. It's an everyday group hallucination. This novel is modeled on that phenomenon. 150 writers, professional and amateur, have contributed to it, not using the mutually blind exquisite corpse method, and not using the "may I have this dance" method where writers take turns being the author, but using the old Hollywood screenwriting system whereby a studio boss had at his disposal a "stable" of writers working simultaneously to crank out a single blockbuster, each assigned specific functions within the overall scheme. The result is generic and perfect. And Reena herself benefits from it by being more of a material entity, a being, than a character—her thoughts and actions are not spanned by any author's mind. Who pulls her strings?

Mama! An author is a routine, which makes for good conversation whenever that routine climbs down from the windswept seclusion that walks and breathes centuries of the word. Fourteen meetings with the publisher it took for this author to become convinced that *Reena Spaulings* was fit for print. Thirty-six bleary-eyed howling dinners of beer and cocaine just to prove that Reena was the product of sweat and tears and frustration. All this drilling, convincing, testing, baiting proves that not only is an author a person who writes, but also a role that is negotiated and trained by those who choose the books one can read today. Becoming an author is a process of subjectivation, and so is becoming a soldier, becoming a cashier, becoming a potted plant.

Like the authors, the New York City depicted herein finds itself constantly exposed to the urges of "communism" – that is, to a chosen indifference to private property, a putting-in-common of the methods and means of urban life and language. Communism, it seems to say, is the only thing we share today, besides our extreme separation. Between the lines is a desire for the not normal situation, a wartime desire not for peace but for a better, fresher war that would produce the not normal situation. In everybody, even an underwear model.

Sometimes, hoping to generate a timely product for young readers today, we couldn't help but produce something unwanted, unexpected instead. *Reena Spaulings* is not the *On The Road* or *The Great Gatsby* of these times, which is to say that these times do not need or want those kinds of books. If the Novel, today, has lost much of its seductive power and its necessity, perhaps we can fill it with something else. This is a novel that could also have been a magazine. It's a book written by images, about images, to be read by other images, which is to say it is uninhibited and realist. Its primary content is the desire to do two things at once: to take something back and to get rid of ourselves. It took us less than three years to write. An impossible book we are now letting go of, so that Reena Spaulings can assume her final pose – along with Tristram Shandy, Edgar Huntly, Effi Briest, Silas Marner, Madame Bovary, Daisy Miller, Moby Dick, and all the others – that of literature.

Reena Spaulings

Chapter 1

Reena is standing, but not sitting. Her hands are behind her, but not in front of her. She's keeping an eye on two rooms at once: the room containing Michiel Sweerts' *Clothing the Naked*, and the one with *Friedland 1807*, the pre-battle panorama of Napoleon's army by Meissonier.

Reena's eyes are brown? Blue? Something like that. Why describe her as beautiful? She's not. She's pre-aesthetic. Meaning there is no man or woman on earth who could say with complacency what it is that makes him or her go back a few steps to see her, or simply what makes him or her see her. What we need is a picture. A poet might have said her nose denoted two conflicting things: independence, and sensuality. And that her eyebrows bespoke female gallantry. But again, how does he or she come up with these conclusions from looking at her? Something in her face said "... ocean... radar." And something in her face and body together said "Trampled Grass." When you actually drive to the prairie. But I don't want to make her out to be more or less or other than human, or even human.

How is she? Young and ugly and beautiful. All-in-one vehicle. A sponge, a vacuum. Strands of not-so-blond hair escaping her barrette. A scouting eye would say... let's get some highlights. Not a wig no, no extensions, no, just a bit of color perhaps, and a brush. Same story with her skin... never seen a facial. Not yet. Not at this point in her life. She knows about these matters, but she doesn't care, nor has she met anybody who made her care or made her want to encounter such improvements. Well, she somehow is required to put her hair out of the face. Because she works in public. And there are rules in a public. But her hair likes to slip. She's somewhat careless with her uniform too. Let me tell you about the uniforms. I was an arthandler for ten years, I rode around in a truck and we picked up paintings and took them around town. There was a guy named Eugene who worked on the trucks and who desired all the other truckers. He would talk filthy to you but very respectfully, which is very pleasant while you're working. Well now he works at the Met as a security guard and I stood up there with him one day while he was on duty. O, I looked at and felt his uniform. He told me what I had heard before, that they were designed by Armani before he was famous. You look at them and you see 'security guard,' 'mild,' 'gentle blue,' 'not very beautiful,' and then that little extra something that you can't put your finger on. Something snazzy but depressed... a Florida wind? "But you better go now because you're distracting me from looking at hot college guys."

Well, Reena stands there with a gold disc on each lapel like all the other guards. They look like toy soldiers, porters, bell-boys, 19th-century things, something snazzy but depressed, controlling yet puppet-like, serving. Serving the world, the museum, the artworks. Serving it up. Their own nothingness, wrapped in a funny costume. A bit scratchy too. All polyester. I love these guards! Waiting, waiting observing. Being magnificently bored. Bearing boredom. What a job! She is not happy, not sad, not nothing. Unuseful servant. You don't need to demonstrate business in that job, but deliver cool static. She is good at that. That's how she got the job in the first place, despite her young age. She has worked here at the museum now for the last seven months. Her sense of listening and her sense of observing with the eye have drastically improved. Super-sensitized, she's become a recording instrument. She knows secrets, she's heard people talk, opinionate, despair: "I don't think she'd understand me"…"what adventures did you have since I last saw you"…"I'd like to live in t-shirt and undershorts"…"How long was I out there crying?"…"Do your best"…"I'm gonna kill this man"… "I love it"… "come on, we all know there will be war." Nobody ever talks in the way it would blow her brains out. Plus she has no desire to interfere with the flows that brought these streams of people, words. It all goes through her now, a surplus of subjectivities at her disposal. Reena, magnificently bored again, all day long.

She knows the grainy surveillance monitors are registering all her moves… sometimes she thought of herself as just a monitor staring back at the other monitors. A Russian man has just asked her where he could find "Broken Eggs," by Jean-Baptiste Greuze, but his party has already found it and is laughing with enthusiasm over this allegory of lost virginity they've come so far to see – the young woman, her basket of eggs upset on the barn floor, the young man with so much extra fabric in his pants, the eggs, the small boy trying to piece one of the eggs back together, the egg running between his fingers, and so forth.

Bernadette, another guard, is two galleries over, also watching her, registering all her moves, and having thoughts about her. Something's different about Reena today, she thinks. Something is making her seem to float there without actually leaving the ground. Bernadette has never exactly gotten to know Reena Spaulings, who always managed to slip into the changing room and punch out before Bernadette had even reached the bottom of the stairs. She wondered if there was something about her that the other guard disliked, or if Reena was just socially awkward. Reena hides behind her bangs. She might be shy or she might just have nothing interesting to say, no ideas. It's true that Reena projected the pre-talkie intelligence of a Lillian Gish or some other silent star. A burlesque intelligence. But Bernadette had ideas. She could manage a stimulating conversation with just about anyone, and liked to ask and be asked penetrating, character-revealing questions. She had a prettier face and much better skin than Reena: you could see Reena's pores up close and pinkish imperfections in the sunlight. Bernadette was also at least an inch taller than the other guard, who compensated with high, non-regulation shoes. Maybe it was the shoes that seemed to be lifting her up on the spot.

The secret behind Bernadette's clear, radiant complexion were the herbal enemas she regularly gave herself. And once a year she went to a Haitian woman in the Bronx and had her colon deep-cleaned, a painful and laborious procedure but definitely worth the trouble. It's amazing what builds up in there. Rotten, clotted matter, and such a pile of it that, after her first visit, Bernadette had made a final decision never to look in that big plastic bowl again at the end of a session, because it disturbed her to know. But the next day her face was as light and clear as a reflection on water and she also felt a lot more positive towards life. Reena was awkward. Think of the waste that's built up in her over the years, the greenish brown muck coating her lower intestine, yards and pounds of it. The lode of waste encrusted into the walls of her colon. To this day Bernadette had never revealed her beauty secrets to anyone and probably never would. It was really nobody's business how she managed her special glow.

Rumors had a way of circulating among the guards. Amy insisted she'd spotted Reena going down on the drummer from The Brown Recluse, who was also a sometime male model, backstage at Waste. But it was pretty dark. Susan thought that Reena was into pills, and was maybe even dealing them on her lunch break and between shifts in Impressionism. That would explain a lot about Reena: her nice shoes, the impenetrable calm she wrapped herself in and that served as an invisible, newspaper-sized barrier between herself and the others, also probably the hovering trick she was performing today over by the Gainsboroughs. But Susan was always talking trash about the other girls and couldn't really back this up. All Bernadette knew for sure were a few details she'd managed to spy on Reena's application form down in Personnel. 23 years old, which made her 24 now. Previous occupation: none. Internship experience at some DIY fashion label. Graduate of a middle-of-the-road arts program somewhere out of state. Other skills: music (guitar), ceramics, fencing, basic French. Arrested twice for disturbing the peace. She could be just about anybody.

Bernadette always made sure to stand on the outside edges of her feet, because another guard had warned her about fallen arches and spider veins. She'd even had special arches custom-made for her work shoes so she could stand for hours without getting very tired. She wondered what Reena looked like with no clothes on. Her breasts were probably cute in a medium sort of way, the kind you could cup in your hand and that wouldn't droop until she was about sixty. Her butt, on the other hand, looked loose on her frame, slightly floppy in her pants. Was she very hairy down there? It was hard to imagine but you could never tell. She imagined Reena as the sort of person who was pretty detached in bed, but once in a while would really let herself go, but extremely. Then she would start using her fists and speaking in tongues. What would it take to get her this way? Probably nothing the other person could think of or do on purpose, maybe the moon on certain months, maybe chemicals. Did she like to have her hair pulled?

Bernadette's mind wandered between her own shoes, the slowly circulating crowd, and her speculations on Reena. Meanwhile her eyes scanned the room methodically, or at least gave the impression of looking around. A high school group was coming down the hall with sketch pads, blocking her view of the Eighteenth Century. She stood up a little straighter and fixed her eyes on a Manet on the opposite wall. The woman in the painting had Reena's blank pallor and below-the-radar presence. Reena could be a Manet, one of these thinking pictures you can't see through, no matter how long you stare at them.

This got Bernadette thinking about herself – that she herself, Bernadette, was no longer quite intact. Down to the very level of her DNA, her double-helix no longer wrapped around itself in some kind of dance but was rather always seeking to escape itself, like a tail running away from its dog. And this had everything to do with the museum. She's worked there for some time already, but this morning, striding through the lobby to her station, she realized that if she were mugged on the street by the museum, she would be hard pressed to pick out her assailant in a police line-up behind a one-way mirror. She's never been able to look at it. Not really.

The Thinker, another guard, a limited man, who'd been here much longer than Bernadette, had once read to her from a small sheaf of papers, clearly part of a larger assemblage, whose neatly written handscript purported to tell a story of his days as a schoolmaster before the war. His words came out in a steady hiss that reminded her of the old steam heating system in her prewar apartment building. "You know what a Leyden jar is it's the classical apparatus for storing electricity, you've seen it over and over again in the laboratory. There was once upon a time a celebrated physicist, a man of science, called Professor Tyndall. He was manipulating a large battery of Leyden jars, while lecturing. Through some carelessness in handling them he received a very severe electric shock. It was so severe it knocked him out. For a few moments Professor Tyndall was insensible. You follow? Well, when Professor Tyndall came to, he found himself in the presence of his audience. There was he, there was the audience, there were the Leyden jars. In a flash he realized perfectly what had happened: he knew he had received the battery discharge. The intellectual consciousness, as he called it, of his position returned more promptly than the optical consciousness. What is meant by that is as follows. He recovered himself, so to speak, very nearly at once. He was conscious on the spot of what had occurred. Professor Tyndall had great presence of mind. He was able to address the audience and reassure it immediately. But *while he was reassuring* the audience, his body appeared to him cut up into fragments. For instance, his arms were separated by his trunk, and seemed suspended in the air. He was able to reason and also to speak as though nothing were the matter. But his optic nerve was quite irrational. It reported every-thing in a fantastic manner. Had he believed what it reported, he would not have been able to address his audience as he did, or in fact address them at all. Do you follow so far? Had it been the optic nerve speaking it would have said, 'As you see, I am all in pieces!' As it was, he said, 'You see! I am uninjured and quite as usual.' Have you followed?"

During this lecture, Bernadette had yawned without intermis-sion. Her yawns had increased in intensity, like the crescendo of howls coming from a dog who is compelled to listen to a musical performance or to sounds above a certain pitch. At length, she remained with her mouth at full stretch, with difficulty getting it closed again as she saw that The Thinker was finishing. Recalling it today however is quite different. There it is. The museum speaks to its audience via its optic nerve after a tremendous trauma. Whether it spoke to itself too in such fashion she was unclear. And whether it even possessed such a thing as an intellectual uncon-scious was for another day. Bernadette, at least, had recollected the story, so she was satisfied that she was in possession of one.

Of course she had seen almost every tiny component of the museum many times over, but all she had were corners, colors, textures, and everything seen with eyes too wide open, with her peripheral vision – in part, she already suspected, not because of some fault of her own, but because the museum itself was in some way homologous to peripheral perception. It barely knew what it was or where. It was the perfect place for breeding speculations.

It reminded her of a conversation she'd had with Josef (pro-nounced *yo-sef*), whom she'd kind of lived with in Berlin, about the first museum ever. But this conversation also involved some details about magpies because there were two magpies on the ground outside the kitchen window where they were talking. Bernadette had remarked how pretty the magpies were and Josef said, "Yes. And they're such horrible birds." He gave some examples of their very spiteful behavior, which he said he never believed when other people told him about it, until he saw it himself. Bernadette said "What about crows." "Crows are wonderful birds." Bernadette had seen the day before on her way home an amazing twilight of crows over a copper building in the middle of town. Josef told her that right behind that building was the first museum that ever was and that it had been designed by Hegel. Only now did she realize he might have been lying, and about other things too. For Bernadette, such ambiguities were the source of a certain stillness, pleasantly unhinged her.

Bernadette checked her watch and saw that it was time to go. She noticed that Reena had already quit her post. As fast as she could go without running, past noblemen, landscapes, still lives, crucifixions and other symbolically-charged scenes, Bernadette made a beeline for the Tapestries. In the stairwell she could hear Reena's leisurely footsteps echoing just ahead of her. She went down the stairs two and three at a time, but when she arrived in the service corridor, Reena was already coming out of the changing room with a maybe-not-even-there smile for Bernadette. Her eyes were bright and her hair looked windblown. Her boy's white oxford shirt was frayed in the collar and in the cuffs, and through it, her purple lace bra was visible. She looked even more perfect than Bernadette had remembered.

"Oh, My God," Rain whispered to Kati in the back of the changing room. "Did she, like, pick up her clothes at a homeless shelter on the way here?" I wonder how many times she's done it, Jenny wondered to herself. She imagined Reena and the drummer/model leaning against a big, black van, his drumsticks jammed in his back pocket. She was very cold, and had got his saliva in her hair, but it was worth it. Then Jenny pictured Reena and another imaginary boy on a ski lift. They began to kiss and couldn't stop themselves. *How cool*, Jenny thought. Hands down, Reena Spaulings was the coolest girl in the entire world.

Chapter 2

PRETTY FACES GOING PLACES

With long dancing strides she makes her way flamboyantly down the street. Her down-cast eyes are a playfully modest reflex borne from her confidence that with her she drags the gazes of the transfixed pedestrian mass.

My ass. I remember walking in Pittsburgh. What a deep, white world those winters were. Coming home from school on darkening afternoons, we took short cuts through alleys that belonged to the Insane Unknowns, a gang we feared but never once saw. Blindness was a part of the urban plan then, as integral to its design as bricks and plate glass, and the few glimpses of evil we actually caught only extended the territories of what stayed invisible. The men who pulled up in cars, a hairy finger on the automatic window button. The guitar solos that oozed out of scary, hippie basements where the bongs were always loaded. Finally back home, my blind mother would be hammering away at Debussy's *The Sunken Cathedral*, with the thermostat always set to a miserly 62 degrees. I remember pyromania, Pennsylvania, geraniums, gymnasiums, head shops, hay rides, hand jobs under the stairs, under the dim, distant stars.

On a small tree-lined street of mild-mannered, bourgeois-brownstone taste, I remember what the two watery globes in the front of my head are for. I am often surprised, not to say a little embarrassed, at how blown-away I can be by the street's beauty after a day in the museum. I see no trace of the grid and am reassured that no such ordering device lies beneath what is. Even the elongated rectangular shapes of the elegant townhouses present themselves as disorderly patchworks of tangents barely touching one another, to say nothing of the mesmerizing rustle of leaves which are like sound shapes increasing and decreasing in volume. Beneath them, the miraculous mechanics of a walking ass.

Buy a Dyptique candle for the bathroom. Moisturizer, bananas, toilet paper. Walking in this city today is more like work on the way home from work. Is there a walking that would be more like giving it all away? My ass, my ass.

79th Street: Where has the day gone? Why does this street never open up? Will I ever kick in a window? And: am I a bisexual? A street of questions. 72nd Street, already: Bodies, outfits, bricks, traffic, traffic reflected in polished granite, glass, cops, bags, voices and horns, a fifty foot-tall athlete wrapping the side of a building, another building shaped like a giant perfume bottle, sliding doors, revolving doors, a sunset about to happen, Reena Spaulings. The smog-loving gingko trees outlasting us all.

Make yourself small. Make yourself the way a small pansy – right now an orange one in one of those small gardens optimistic people plant around the base of a tree is reaching towards me – can somehow be larger, in some strange internal trick of perspective, than the hulking presence of the tree which dwarfs us both. This is a property not of the flower, nor of mine alone, but it is induced by my capacity, my power, to reduce my size. In order to redistribute size and attention like this, Reena realized that her size, her speed, and her location were analogous in some way to the properties of wavelengths and their waves.

Dogs, apparently devoid of color sensors, were virtually blind in comparison to the way Reena felt herself moving towards this flower now – they sought always to make themselves larger by barking, the land equivalent of dolphins' sonar navigation, but she liked dogs anyway, because they didn't consider themselves larger than the tiny olfactory particles whose smelly trails they slavishly follow. What power of identification was in operation here, that a dog could reduce itself to the size of a particle in order to befriend, follow, chase and terrorize these odors? Her conclusion was that a dog must have a way of perceiving itself at such a great distance in time or space and realizing itself *there* at the size of a particle, rather than where it was, at the size of a hairy flea-bag. A dog chasing its tail is not an imbecile, but a physician of genius, chasing itself in and out of scales of magnitude. She was walking in the wavelengths of color beyond color.

Smell the concrete, steel, metal parts, debris of today, debris of tomorrow. To hell with a structure. Hell, you people. She did not like standing still for hours after hours. She liked moving softly. Mobility and illusion: her tools, her hope, her dream of making a dream possible again. 66th Street: The feeling that something might explode.

Here, life resembles the part of the fashion magazine that suddenly addresses the reader face to face, so to speak, or as one knowing girlfriend to another. Here, life and bodies are as clean and organized as a magazine, picture perfect. Who do you love? How do you love? I am continuously killed by love. In bed, in the street, in the movies. I'm addicted to maximum exposure and maximum identification with whatever touches me, a conspiracy involving myself and everything. Is that love? Over coffee, people urge me to get my thing together. Rickety, demented banjo music is coming out of the speaker. I am in there somewhere, coming out too, blasting it. I have never felt more open to anything. Meanwhile, at a table nearby, a conversation about Modernist color theory, the Bauhaus, color wheels, Joseph Albers...

Page 129: a glowing skinned girl in a pristine white tank top, summery sarong, and flip flops sits on a sidewalk bench drinking fresh fruit juice and talking into her cell phone. Page 84: all the outdoor tables of the neighborhood café are filled with good-looking, cargo-panted creative types lounging away the afternoon. The trees, bodies, small designer-ish boutiques, the neighborhood atmosphere, the sun, form so many idyllic scenes. In each, the morality of plump skin and healthy bodies, the uniformity of laid-back stances, and lips that redundantly pronounce individual lifestyle preferences... exactly like magazine copy. Scream of a mind: I need money, give me money! Stupid girl.

Breaking her nose once in London trying to cross Oxford Street. Looking right, then left. Aware of the traffic. Spotting an opportunity to cross, stepping off the high curb while looking right, her right foot describing an arc up, falling down, providing a route into which all the weight of her body rushed, her head turning back to the left, seeing too late that a small old man had appeared in front of her, his temple met by her head with all the force familiar to those who sit in the end of a roller coaster, seeing him fall to the ground. In cartoons, one sees brightly colored stars in such circumstances. In hospitals, she ponders, one cannot see the color which slides straight through her make-up, her skin, her eyes, paints the inside of her head, her broken nose. The ability of the short and energetic x-ray wavelength to pass through obstacles – alternatively its *inability* to rest, to lazily and gloriously pool itself on a surface – was what excited her about color. And these qualities of different wavelengths were like a book of strategies for her: to pass through solid objects, or to decorate surfaces.

Everything here is heavily sooted. The massive boulevard is a horizontally coursing field of metal, machine, impatience, bouncing rubber, aggression, exhaust fumes, horns, sirens, and bass. The turning red of the traffic light – whereupon a segment slams to a stop just short of the crosswalk – effects rhythmic gouges in the consistency to let pedestrians through. Where does my (boyish, jaunty, smooth, freckle-dusted, foxy, stiff, screen-like) body end and a real event begin, for once? A body is a living, breathing image that thinks while exposing itself to others. An event is like a place where two or more bodies become mutually exposed, reach a certain a degree of improvisation and contamination. What if nothing belonged to anybody?

The machines of the heavy asses, lifted and moved one cheek at a time, the machines of incessantly moving jaws and snapping gum; packs of teenage boys who give forth exclamatory bursts of sound; breasts in tight sport jerseys; buttocks in tight denim; bouncing shoulders in soft leather; and the traffic of shouting voices. And then there are immobile things like dangling street signage, fire hydrants, and rusted garbage cans, and 'painfully broke' stores whose merchandise is more assaulting than seductive. She was drifting into one of those spaces that barely exist: spaces that are created by beautification and pedestrian control projects which, when one steps into such a useless nook or cranny, are filled suddenly with the melancholy of a Western ghost town, redundant in the wake of the new railroad.

A sliver, twisted pipe. Out of commission. A foot in diameter, it's thick and disturbing to look at. It's lying along the sidewalk for about 12 feet. It twists at 4 joints, like a robot snake frozen in mid-writhe. It's hollow inside and makes a "bongk" sound. Inside, its walls are thick with some sort of blackened buildup. Sitting on it can give a feeling of sitting on a fallen tree trunk on a tropical island, until it starts to suck the heat out of your rear and you know there's no way you could be at the beach.

Reena fastened a grip on a lamppost and hoisted herself up onto an electrical box hidden amongst the flower beds to get a better view, to sight land. From her crow's nest, peering across the vast vistas of the Avenue, she was astonished to see with the greatest clarity, other islands amidst the seas. Most were uninhabited. But on one, a small movement gave away another human under a weight of gray cloth and dirty plastic. On another, a taxi driver pulled a letter from a bottle washed up and caught in his net of windscreen wipers, though he did not appear either excited or pleased at this miracle. On yet another, volcanic eruptions as a middle-aged couple argued, heatedly. But she was no Robinson Crusoe. She cursed the sunshine for hiding the positions of the stars and forcing her to make do with *Bud Lite*, *Oyster Club*, and *CitiBank*.

A deep breath and a push, and she was out again on the frothy mixture. Then she was being fairly whipped along in a current of gray Italian cotton, too fast, too turbulently to develop an exit strategy, feeling depressed. Rage rising. Rage ebbing. There was what she called malaria of the soul. The total being is one large breeding ground for the shocks of the world past, present, future. All living and dying, all vibrations pass through her and over her. Annihilate her. It comes and goes whenever it likes. It rules her, commands her, envelops her, everywhere and all the time. It bloweth where it listeth. It sucks her up and grows through her. In the spine, in the brain, in the blood, in the guts. Is it love?

Finally 14th Street: It's an attraction to something that gives a person their shape, a life its form. A lifestyle is defined by taste, or even by a taste for absence, but a life-form, here in the city or wherever, happens when a body is affected by an attraction. And whatever a body leans toward also leans toward it. So a life-form is something between bodies, in every situation, and is always new each time. These inclinations are reciprocal and improvised and intense.

The blue-jeaned tourists, have gone. Taxis have spread to the strips along the East and West Sides. Younger men rush to meet their mothers. Doormen laze in their thresholds. You are taking care of business after a weekend of deserved rest, perhaps Upstate, or after the movies. Outside the Henry James brownstones on the north side of the park, teenage couples stroll towards Broadway, towards the subways that will take them back to Queens or Harlem or somewhere. Certain couples fight or brag. A girl swings her purse at her boyfriend, who ducks between a parked Volvo and a newspaper box. Neither suspect that under its heaps of ransacked bulletins the box contains fifteen tin-foiled cakes of pinkish Ecstasy, placed there at dawn by a middle-aged white drifter in the employ of Jamaican drug workers. Reena had somehow lined up all her particles in the same line, positive and negative charges in order, such that she was moving through the city in the way that power flows across an imbalance in charge – she had been navigating by polarities, across voids even, and would arrive at a spot, or at least be in movement towards that spot even before a conscious decision to get there could articulate itself.

Prince Street: You can use other citizens as shields to block the cameras and mirrors. Take your time, relax. Peel off the magnetic sticker thing while keeping your eyes up on the shelves, just browsing. I fill my pockets with Dr. Hauschka's face milk, Uncle Grimes' old fashioned tooth powder, a sponge made out of a real sponge from the sea, tea tree oil impregnated toothpicks, lavender scented roll-on deodorant. Only the best.

If what we mean when we say lifestyle is a leaning into programmed nothingness, a life-form is like a line of increased and increasing potential, distinct from any other line in a situation. If only I could find my line and follow it. If my life-form were that of a warrior, for example, everything I touched would be immediately transformed into a weapon. Or if it were a priest's, everything I touched would become a prayer. To follow my line and abandon myself to the process that is my form-of-life. A life-form is a process that elaborates me, and that I abandon myself to.

In the window of Dean & Deluca, on the left, is a display of about seven human forms, momentarily evacuated. Whatever qualities or functions normally animate them, the coffee break has unplugged them from it, leaving slack postures in a raincoat, leather briefcase, beige skirt, flower-patterned pants, crew neck sleeveless pullover, jean jacket, and camel-colored boots. With hands about the gray and white cups, seven pairs of eyes, seven heads, seven haircuts, seven current-less bodies, their fronts pressed against the glass, all gaze. My ass.

Sexedup, sexeddown, whatever.

I climb two flights of stairs. No Jonas. No Nathan, Jason, Priscilla. And again two flights. No cats. No cat food. Is it that I forgot or that I didn't want to buy any. Two flights again. I will not play "shopping ass" to Antonio's "glad and sad" shop-owning ass. "Do you know how to make potato soup?" Mom had said. I was happy and didn't know how to, and still don't. Tonight I will sup on nuts, and a squid salad. Sixth floor: Hi Mark-Andy, Hi, top of my building. Hi door, Jonas. I kiss you all. Hail, pink plastic trash on floor, a kiss to you via my hand. Hallway, and long block of air, hi, a kiss to you and a visit soon. Books, TV, laptop, napkins, backgammon board, hi, and fuck you. Hail, floor. Chairs and futon, hail and fuck you. I'll soon sit on you. Nudity. Taking off my shirt. Untying hair. Pissing, washing. No calls. Should I go out tonight? Try not to flip out at Liz's party as you did last March.

Three cop cruisers sitting in a row, showing only profile. Headlights poke out one from behind the other. They are navy blue with white letters. The occupants of the cars are not visible. But they must be there, the cars are idling. White exhaust breaks up out of their tailpipes. They are sitting below a dark overhang over which a sign reads, "Midtown Packing." One of the cop cars pulls out like a silent shark, and after a moment all of them are gone.

Chapter 3

THE THRESHOLDS

O n the outside, Waste still looked like the fishermen's supply
shed it had once been way back in Herman Melville's time.
Getting in was as simple as knowing whose name to mention at the
door: "Debbie Mayfield." Crossing the dark entry and on through
a low arched way, cut through what in old times must have been a
great central chimney with fire-places all round, you entered the
main upstairs party room, dark, with such low beams above and
such old wrinkled planks beneath that you would almost think you
trod some old craft's cockpits on a howling night. On one side
stood a long low, shelf-like table covered with glasses and cracked-
open cases of beer. Projecting from the far angle of the room was a
dark-looking den – the bar, behind which bustled a withered man
selling the girls and boys their deliriums.

Distracted by a guy she once dated making out with a girl she
used to share a studio with, Reena stumbled in the entryway and
scraped her face either on a rusty nail or on somebody's long
fingernails as they tried to break her fall. Then she lost her one
twenty-dollar bill under some feet in the dark. On her hands and
knees, she was trying to recover the money but lost an earring in
the process. The twenty dollars weren't so important but the earring
was sentimental. She waited at the bar, dabbing her face with a
paper napkin until it stopped bleeding. At least her drinks would be
free tonight.

She noticed the place had been repainted in the style of certain late Francis Picabias. Depicted in muddy browns and mossy greens, sad and startled women's faces were superimposed with birds, guns, ships and bowls of fruit. A black vagina-shaped hole or eye was splitting the sky open in the background of one of the wall paintings. Reena stared at this last detail for a long time, and every so often a bright, but alas, deceptive idea would dart through her – It's the Black Sea in a midnight gale. – It's the unnatural combat of the four primal elements. – It's a blasted heath. – It's a Hyperborean winter scene. – It's the breaking-up of the ice-bound stream of Time. But at last all these fancies yielded themselves back to that one portentous something in the picture's midst. *That* once found out, all the rest would be plain. The place looked much better before when the only decoration to speak of was a winking, blinking, dusty, year-round Christmas tree. As always, she had to look around to find the way downstairs, down to the party behind the party beneath the party.

At the bottom of a long flight of concrete steps (whose entrance was curtained with a net of army vehicle camouflage) was a room of dressed masonry out of which several archways stretched, forming an al-Queda-like underground party-maze. In the hallways the music from the medium-sized rooms containing the bars and DJs was only a faint murmur and the speakers out here/there played a soundtrack consisting exclusively of the summery sounds of crickets. The central room was painted black and against the wall opposite the steps was a long row of cheap vinyl restaurant chairs whose tall backs had been tranformed into gravestones, Magik Markered with the names and life spans of various deceased ex-regulars: Lil' Nut 1971–1999, Tweetie 1968–2001, Kurt Kokaine 1975–2003, Karin E. Glabb 1982–2004, Stubbs 1819–1929, etc. Sparsely lit and with a number of TV monitors showing videos ranging from amateur Mexican bull riding to a film of a Mick Jagger-in-the-early-seventies look-alike putting his dick through the window of a subway booth (onto the attendant on the other side), the locale made for slow navigation. There is no DJ in this room. He is upstairs, on the second floor, alone, named Sunny, in a brightly lit room, with beer cans. His bright music is being pumped down to this basement cave, two levels below the main floor.

After dodging a dancing Paris Hilton look-alike with no arms to pick up a few free drinks at the bar, Reena sat down on a low bench in one of the narrow hallways, next to a group of French guys wearing home-customized jeans of the kind girls in dancehall videos used to wear, facing a video about a rowdy group of fashion models on a camping trip. They had lost their way and were trying to build a makeshift shelter in a storm. Cut to a close-up of a waifish boy screaming into the camera with terrorized abandon. The camera pulls back to reveal his broken body lying at the bottom of a pile of loose boulders. He can't move but he can sure scream. A jagged leg bone has pierced his plaid pants. Reena did not yet know she was watching a Maris Parings production, the first of the rising culture-preneur's silent club-films, a cheap but slick genre of her own invention and a clever way of keeping her boys in the spotlight in slow times. Fade to a Freddie Mercury-in-the-early-80's look-alike playing frisbee with a Labrador retriever, wearing very short shorts. The camera follows the frisbee as it sails out of view, into a dark forest at the edge of the field.

Tonight the party is in full effect. You know this immediately. A party like this one has a very simple graph to it. In about an hour, or two at the most, people will be vomiting, but now, in this particular party room, this appendix, people are euphoric.

"Will someone please stand up?" (Reena was talking to Peter Janovins.) "The man in the back there, will you please stand up. I felt she was talking to me but I didn't want to assume. She was in on my energy, which made me feel dishonest. And it is essentially dishonest to have an energy. Will the blond man in the back part of the theater stand up, with the thinning hair... Now, I liked her very much, I liked everyone in there. Nipples. I stood up and left. If it ever happens again I would like to stand up and not leave. But with my energy, which she was picking up on, I had to either leave or lose that energy, which is hard to do. The energy was, I was liking them. There's really no sticking around, with that energy. So I got up and went to pee, and never saw them again."

Smoke, perfumes and body odor. Girls, competing crazily for attention, drugs, jobs, beauty. Luck was on Reena's side. At least in her vicinity. She's not the frozen statue tonight. She is shiny hair. A new product brushed into it before setting off to the party. A dress borrowed from one of her model-girlfriends, who has made a name for herself as the toughest party girl and was now trying to figure out how to translate this into becoming-an-actress. A room packed with ambition. There is a hat too, and it's too warm to wear a hat. But she is not someone who corrects herself easily. It's a take it or fuck you attitude. She wears it like an invisible armour…every party is a battle. Will she get out of here alive?

The party was reaching the level of panic of good times, which is the only comfortable level for a party-in-itself, when it can know it is alive, although the people in the party are not accorded any special knowledge of whether they are alive or not, or happy or not. The people in the party are swept into an orgy of considerations about the other people in the party, into lubricated thought. The panic of good times is something that draws people into it, and flees from them, hence the panic, which is later remembered as a good time. Reena told Peter Janovins her dream about going up to Anchorage, Alaska at great expense. "Like a salmon," said Peter. A girl named Heather was fighting her way upstream, exuberant, belligerent, toward the drink table, in a tube top. Her breasts rubbed against Reena's and Peter's backs and elbows in passing. "Who *assed* you?" said Jonathan Martiniss to someone behind him. Jonathan was a man with two eyes pointing in slightly different directions, which gave him an air of being untouched by psychology.

Reena wanted to crawl under the crowd, pull its weight onto her like a blanket and fall asleep there. She closed her eyes and floated in its noise – sea water lapping against rocks made of skin and rubber, pierced through now and then by a wheezing, Peckinpah cackle from the end of the bar. There was also the distant sound of fox hunting horns being piped in over the speakers. The music was both aristocratic and barbaric and summoned up images of blood-splattered cashmere and tweed. When Reena looked again she was staring into an urgent, chattering, red-nosed face, a W.C. Fields-from-the-30's look-alike who had his leg cocked up on a black air purifier.

Black three-foot-high candles in tall glass beakers trimmed with peacock feathers and fragrant white orchids flickered every-where. Jenny had never seen anything this cool in her life. "God, I don't know anyone here," she said nervously. Roberto nursed an aching testicle while talking to Jim about Odile. Dan felt like Cinderella. He shoved his hands in his pockets to keep them from shaking, and tried to plan his next move. He would walk over and suavely offer to buy Semanta a drink. Too bad the only suave thing about him was his outfit. Even it was only half as suave as it could have been if he'd kept the Ungaro from Barney's. "Hey," Dan said when he reached their table, his voice cracking. "Hey Dan," Semanta said, "nice tux." The rumors couldn't possibly be true. Semanta didn't look like the sex-crazed drug-addicted maniac Maris had made her out to be. She looked delicate and perfect and exciting, like a wildflower you stumble upon unexpectedly in Central Park.

Reena fell in and out of conversations. Two different people told her the slapstick joke about the blonde who walked into a library by mistake. Then she was being physically moved across the room and into the far corner by a sort of invisible undertow. She landed next to Isabelle, the Swiss exchange student who was always everywhere these days, always all in black and always in the corner. Isabelle was going on about "human money," saying how the kids' bodies were like dollars circulating in an open market, how even the most destitute and threadbare of them carries himself into the night like a millionaire or some sort of walking business-or-pleasure proposal, etc, and how this was maybe the secret of their undeniable beauty as well… Her voice came out in a thin warble, a weak and broken signal coming through under the fox horns. Reena moved closer to catch her words, bending her ear to the slowly moving lips.

A big, unspoken issue at the party was money. It was a kind of boundary line that everyone respected. A line of mutual unkindness. This is where my money ends and yours begins. There were people who had it and didn't care about it, people who were acquiring it and didn't care about it, people who cared and were not in the act of acquiring it, who didn't have it and didn't care, who cared and had it, and so on.

Then Reena was enjoying the sensation of walking in a garden of talking, kissing, smiling and serious mouths. The toothless, cackling cowboy mouth at the end of the bar was still erupting every few minutes in the most surprising way. She was surrounded by mouths and could feel their warm breath on her face. They were little wet caves. She wanted to stick her fingers into them, or nipples or coins. Mouths everywhere, opening and closing. She noticed one with hardly any lips at all, just like Irm Hermann, her favorite Fassbinder actress. Reena loved to look at mouths because to her they were like eyes looking at hers. She looked at their mouths with her own Pasolini mouth, and she sometimes ended up swimming in spit at the end of the night. She couldn't tear herself away from mouths.

The sound of the party was rising now, and supporting itself, like a fire. Anyone who spoke had to refer his or her voice up to the general ball of sound and let it bounce back down. "You look mad." "I look Mad?" "And bored." "Ha ha ha. That's a damn shame, mad and bored!"

Here was a woman whose skin was powdery and soft, an opaque, Shiseido-coated shield. Against this pure field her over-glossed lips stood out almost like a... like pussy lips. Speaking as a man, it was the most vaginal effect possible in a face, but still they were perfectly pretty, perfectly formed, classical lips with their corners almost imperceptibly upturned. Their obscenity was all in the application of the gloss, its slick film bleeding ever so slightly over the actual edges of the lips and onto the powdery skin, extending the mouth beyond itself, unleashing it in simulated wetness. This gave the impression of a mouth just kissed, or having just sucked somebody off, or even a mouth asleep, or a sleeping vagina. Her cool, subliminal smile, on the other hand, confounded this suggestion with something haughty and impassive. It was very effective, this collision between brainless cocksucker and imperious manageress. The one and only Maris was at Waste tonight.

Presently a just-photographed head jerked around in surprise. The photographer gave a cheerful nod equivalent to a thumbs up.

Reena saw beautiful men. My god, angels, burning bright. You just wanted to take their pants down. Velvety genitals all in one. So great to see sexy friends. Like violets growing on a little bank together. Of course they grew that way together. Lilies-of-the-valley. Their hair, their talk, was theirs. Who tasted one tasted the other. Boy-friends.

She tries to get her hand on this pretty boy, obviously fucked with a zillion times recently, flirting like a manic rabbit with all the beautiful girls and even the not so beautiful ones. Soft-spoken and slightly druggy looking with that intentionally slightly greasy hair curving in his face. There was a certain amount of drippy openness to this guy, but some notion of lost drama too. Her girlfriends had lost their opinions when it came to this one. They were through with him and he with them already over and over again. She had never been attracted by the game, but in this case it seemed it was failure, the being-thru-ness, that made the boy attractive. He had been through everything and was still open and searching? But to what ends? Reena tried to figure out the possibilities of generating something unexpected in this encounter... but couldn't see it yet.

Then her drink was gone and she was sharing his. Then his double-jointed fingers were snaking their way under Reena's dress as she tried to climb his narrow body like a tree. Isabelle wagged her head in despair and was now going around the room starting small fires with a cigarette lighter. All the fires were stomped out by laughing friends until the girl gave up and fell asleep with her face buried in Semanta's lap. As Reena crossed the room, laughing out loud, Maris Parings reached out and stabbed her bottom with a lit Marlboro Light.

"Ha. Ha. Ha. Ow! Wow, bitch...!"

Maris wasn't sure what had made her want to burn Reena. She tried to behave apologetically and fished an ice cube out of her glass.

"Oh dear, I don't know how that happened. Here..."

Reena let this thirty-something woman rub her down there with the ice cube. It was a slightly embarrassing spectacle that froze her on the spot.

"I was watching you before. You're having fun."

Reena was out of words.

"You're kind of cute, but you don't have a lot going on up there do you?" said Maris pointing at Reena's messy hair.

Reena helped herself to one of the woman's cigarettes and lit the wrong end of it.

"I like your face."

Somebody's coat was smoldering under the table, sending whiffs of burnt nylon into Reena's tired, smiling face. She was suddenly in the mood to befuckedintheass, but not by any of these citizens in particular. Lizzi was sleeping in broken glass, her tongue slightly protruding while an off-duty cop prodded her with the tip of his Reebok, wanting to know who would be paying for all the damage. Without looking up, Maris Parings surrendered her credit card.

Reena started to leave the room. There was a half slap-happy air in the way she moved her body forward, ready to bump into something. The fox horns seemed to clear a path between the bar area and the bathrooms, and Maris followed her down it with her glass of ice cubes. People were lounging in the anterooms like so many cats with hair on their heads. A wave of snappy, small rhythms was apparently following Reena, reading her body, making her almost turn around. All rattling cubes and clattering heels, Maris finally threw her body into a plush banquette and wondered where the girl would disappear to next. "How many of us," she thought, "it takes to change a light bulb into a flickering light bulb." Only the people under 5 feet tall could feel the breeze from an open door glide around their necks.

There was Reena again, coming out of the bathroom with a long piece of toilet paper trailing from her shoe. "I'll take that," said Maris. She took a fast step forward, jumping through the crowd, viciously forcing a heel of her sandal through the paper trail. What was it about Reena that was already erasing the other girls – Blair, Jane, Barbara, Ludmilla, Hanna, Nebraska, Ines – from her mental Polaroid file? This was large; Maris's thrill would not soon subside as she entertained the question Reena seemed to inhabit: genius or idiot? The ambiguity of her attitude drove Maris crazy, and that ambivalent hair even more so. If you could turn a person over and over in your mind like a pig over an open flame, that's what Maris had been doing with Reena for the past forty minutes. Her ice cubes had long since turned to water. Her mind boiling over, thoughts attached like sticky wings.

Just then two muscle-bound men were muscling their way into the banquette with Maris. Reena was watching frankly. She could not get enough of that view, intensified by stroboscopic spasms of light from the dance floor. "We just won a body building contest," they shouted over the music, "Look, our picture is in the paper!" Maris was like a sardine between two potatoes, and her mood floated and splashed like water on these glistening rocks. How to get through it now, should I embrace it all, including the steamy muscle-men? The two men were unzipping their nylon gym bags which were crammed with newspaper clippings, shining trophies, and several zip-lock baggies containing what looked to Reena – she was riveted now, approaching – like cocaine. Reena's proximity and interest was to Maris nothing less than a wish come true. So there was only one thing left to do: the first line together. "We're so psyched," the largest of the men told Maris. "You have to help us celebrate. We don't know anybody here," said the other.

A cloud of sweat hovered above the dance floor. Newcomers kept bursting through the doorway, eager to immerse themselves. A woman pushed through the crowd with her hands on the waist of her friend ahead. Party train, chugging through.

"WE'RE SO WET!!!" they drunkenly scream in unison, totally aware of absolutely everything in the world.

The voices commingle, making a body of their own, which clamors higher and higher, out-climbing the music even. It leaves down below the darkened figures to their limited gestures and facial expressions, making its own lively party overhead.

"All this spread out momentarily for you to gaze at."

"Do you have another candle for our table?"

A few, who find themselves talking with someone they adore, enjoy the conditions of having to bring their mouth into the loved one's hair, nestling right up to the ear to speak there, in that little private zone of warmth. And then the reciprocal pleasure of having the other do the same to them, tingly breath against their ear which we call lovers' telephone.

Maris and Reena were perched on the bodybuilders' steely laps. The crowd was pushing up, but allowed this fateful conference its very own tiny island in the alcoholic haze. They were leaning into each other now, their words lost to everyone but themselves.

"The only interest that penetrates us because of its own death."

Chapter 4

O nce it had appeared in her life it would never leave again, as
obvious as it is unexplained, neither ugly nor beautiful, escaping all judgements: a solemn sign, who knows, of a superiority? A
superiority but not a stability. One of the most beautiful things
there is. Most open. Most mysterious at the same time. A tough
portrait. A mess. A confusion of signs. A simultaneous affirmation
and negation of lust and life. It is a weird painting, a dream and a
manifestation, composed out of elements that seem not to belong
together. They form a gaze, an intense, worldly but not sexy, scru-
tinizing tough picture of a woman. It is hanging in a corner in the
museum, department of 19th-century French painting, Edouard
Manet, oil on canvas, 1866: *Young Lady in 1866.*

Reena's on her feet again, presiding over the meeting between
people and pictures of people. She's still a little lost in the after-
effects of last night's musclemen and their drugs. A pleasant, run
over by tires feeling. If called on to speak she would have trouble
doing so. The paintings seem to be getting what they need, and the
people are heavy, drowsy in the galleries today. A young Japanese
couple is drifting through, laughing, brushing, crushing each other's
clothing. An American bald man seems to follow, or drift along in
their wake.

Violets in hand, she looks like an appropriated renaissance
madonna. A fallen, half-peeled orange lies at the bottom of a stand

upon which the parrot is sitting. In front of the parrot is a glass with water for him to drink. The woman is standing against a dark blackish-green background. Her dress is huge, covering her entire body with salmonish-pink satin. It is quite a contrast. One notices right away the other black parts in the portrait, as they seem to be the connecting agents to that abstract plane: one tip of a foot stepping out of the pink, the black velvet choker round her neck, and her eyes. There is also the parrot's one eye.

Reena stations herself in the carnival route, where people come out from the Degas room all turned on and fly by Manet to get to Courbet. That seems to have been the idea, she meditates, to have Courbet's naked *Woman with a Parrot*, also 1866, right at the end of the arcade, a destination. This woman sprawls on her back laughing, flirting with her own bird, who is on her finger flapping his wings, seemingly maddened by the acre of hair that flows from her head. What's her body to him? Her nipples. Reena is still tasting the cocaine, and in her own hair smells cigarettes from last night and the oil from the musclemen's biceps.

She's starting to fall asleep on her feet while guarding. It's something every guard has done, and knows how to do. She starts running back snippets from last night. Sometimes she unintentionally makes a face while standing there, or speaks a little by surprise in response to her memories. Not even memories but actual odors. Manet's *Young Lady in 1866* stands near Reena, inhaling from her purple nosegay something that seems to be dilating her. She's with her parrot. They're not playful adversaries, but "of a mind." She, the parrot, and the half-peeled grapefruit down in the bird gravel like a cracked open head. A precise life-form.

Her eyes are somewhat piercing. But she doesn't attack. She is waiting. One hand holding the violets, the other playing casually with a small looking-glass that dangles from her neck. Her dress has big buttons, also covered with cloth. She is fearlessly looking straight at us, although her head is painted slightly at an angle, a

3/4 view. The girl that modeled was a favorite of that era. Very full of herself. She could take weird costumes as well as nakedness. She is very different from other girls. Slightly detached, containing some knowledge but no divine mysteries. She is not a radiant beauty here. A woman weirdly packaged into this ambiguous dress. Some kind of underwear, but not really. A robe for the morning hours. A house robe to receive guests in or to wear in solitude. A protecting device. Or she might be pregnant. Its enormous volume of cloth matches the tones of her head and hands, and the effect of this unites the composition. Even more, it pushes the painting into something emblematic, makes it the even more unshakable icon. You go there and you might wanna stick your head in the folds of that pink-flesh-cloth, lick the black boot and expose yourself to the tough stream of thought emanating from her stare.

Some of whatever happened at Waste eludes Reena's memory of the night before. Like the dark parts in the Manet, these gaps are the connecting agents to the abstract plane she calls "good times." They are the not so good times, or the times in-between, the parts that contrast with the fun, pink, fleshy areas that unite the composition of her conscious experience of the party. She remembers the sexy, almost scary proximity of Maris's glossy lips, but not what they said. She remembers that at one point the musclemen had challenged each other to a bench-pressing contest, using her and Maris's bodies as weights. But not what caused the commotion afterwards, or how she ended up alone in the street. She remembers the cab ride home, but not how she paid for it.

The image of the peeled orange (in classic 17th century still life ensembles it is often a lemon) is an emblem of vanitas painting, although here it is painted as unassumingly as a Chardin. The looking glass is really a monocle and it must have been a gift from a guy, as women did not wear these things around their necks in those days. It implies the presence of or a recent visit from a fashionable man. Whatever that means. Did he leave this object to mark his territory? But she doesn't stay there. She makes use of the given thing, the given situation, the painting.

She knows we know she's being watched, and painted, and she is playing a part. It is a lot of small mental and murky movements, frozen in action, stuffed in a darkened background. A figure with odd things, accessories of a situation. And then there is the clumsy openness of her hand. Those painted fingers holding a bundle of violets close to the head, nose. The violets were also a gift. Now she is smelling them, female smelling. Painting unravels as an illusion and unpeels as a situation. The illusion unravels like in a Warhol, leaving something that's not an illusion. Clothing remains on importantly. All five senses formally addressed. And there is also the talking bird, the pet parrot, the other voice, a truth, a trash-talking guy, before the era of the telephone.

Reena is standing on her feet not sitting, with her hands behind her back. Fox hunting horns are trumpeting in the distance in her head, another echo of Waste, like the odors, not yet a memory, a lingering actuality. She is not conscious of this music. She is looking at the *Young Lady in 1866*'s fingernails. Manet never painted fingernails but we see them anyway.

Here is observing for those who can no longer see. Or for those who can't really look into another person's eyes. A painting something like a practicing ground: Learn to hold a gaze. To look at this painting is to experience a situation sensuously rich and extremely suggestive, yet not real at all. A special fiction to inhabit. Another kind of performance unfolding, making room for fantasies now, and narratives full of intimacies. The dressing gown becomes flesh armor. Her head is sitting on top with her eyes dark holes dragging you into some kind of involvement. Perhaps flirtatious. Then take the painting from behind. Think that.

I once looked at a snapshot of myself in Salzburg on a bridge, posing next to a large poster of my friend Rich. The poster happened to be there, and it was the phoniest thing, his mustache, his shirt. All around it were the river, a cliff surmounted by a castle, other stone bridges, people, cars… but that poster was the realest, most alive thing in the snapshot. Double phoney has a greater reality than stones, rivers.

The most substantial thing in this painting is the odor of the violets. She is more aura than substance, as the substance of desire eludes possession. She embodies the role of the object of the gaze that his representations of her hold or suspend in the very act of looking. There is an encompassing solitude at the heart of this exchange. Painting's self-reflexivity is that which most solicits the enjoyments of the senses of sight, smell and touch, and just as powerfully turns back into paint. She is a painting on the verge of breaking out into a different style (and a different woman). Her name is Victorine Meurent. A working class girl and Manet's favorite model in the 1860s. Painter and model are fixing a gaze so much until it breaks, identities break down, mind-blur, not yet visible but about to happen. She was paid to do that. Irredeemable, she was enjoying herself standing.

Reena has a blackish-green bruise on her thigh where one of the musclemen, in a moment of excitement or panic, had fastened his gorilla grip. Somebody's phone number is inscribed upon her palm, half-erased there in the chemical sweat. Reena is drifting in and out of consciousness while standing and looking at Mlle. Meurent.

There's a promise somewhere in the dark, as well as in the abstract flesh-cloth of becoming, for a woman, to get out of yourself. Playing a part, messing up a part. Now you are ready for arising curiosity, perhaps even emotions, made out of rewritings of identities via the aesthetic materials of clothing, make-up, paint and so on. To enter a room, to look at a painting, you don't even need a dark room. It can be all out there, and always on. The pleasure of stupidizing.

"Now," it occurs to Reena, "I'm ready to extend the domain of pleasures."

She likes the title *Young Lady in 1866*. Imagine the Degas drawing being called *Woman Drying Her Arm in 1884*. She thinks about this particular young lady modeling in 1866. The painting "threads the needle" for Reena. It remains a painting and rides a thin line into her brittle subway thoughts. And forcing a plaster cup, fully she'll keep this spot after lunch. She's drifting off. America George Washington on the shores, ... score up on the strings... Reena is asleep standing.

z z z

Maris Parings tied a small, quivering dog to a parking meter, gave it a kiss on the nose, and breezed in through the museum's doors. Reena saw her gliding past the Gainsboroughs as if on little wheels. What was she doing here, and in the same soiled dress from the night before? Bernadette observed the meeting from her post, saw their hands in each other's hands, their cheeks against each other's cheeks. Maris Parings was not here for the art. She slipped Reena a business card and was pointing at her organizer with a flexing vine of a finger. Her eyes were swimming all over Reena's uniform and behind each smile she had another one waiting in reserve.

The idea was to use Reena for a fashion shoot, a last-minute brainstorm on Maris's part, and she was more than willing to break her contract with Women because she was so sure that Reena's gawky, asymmetrical physique, day-old-bread skin (blemishes included), and somewhat lost-looking face would really make the underwear come alive this season.

This campaign would be their best ever, and would speak to a generation long numbed by swollen breasts and lips, jutting hips, machine-flattened tummies and picture-perfect hair. The fall-winter line would hit the market with a poetic-realist slant, and the bras and panties would come off even sexier if the body wearing them wasn't so over-determined in advance by the product it modeled. It would have the energy of an encounter, and would therefore involve people and produce a more exciting, even catastrophic relationship between the skin and eye. The images would reinvent Reena as a knockout, in her own way, the kind that nobody saw coming. But most exciting of all, we would be making that once-in-a-generation leap into a seemingly unknown form of seduction. We will use very little make-up and flat, natural lighting. It will be photographed by that upstart son of a gun dealer, Bjärne Mayhem. If his naked party polaroids no longer wowed the art world, his almost-naked billboards might still cause a car crash or a crush or whatever.

Reena shrugged her shoulders and looked not entirely moved by the proposal. She deliberated for a long minute, shooting glances at the taut flanks and shining eyes of a Reynolds horse (*Scared by Lightning*) as she thought it over. She couldn't help wondering if Maris was insane. As soon as she got her yes, Maris was gliding out again, past a curious Bernadette and into the throbbing spring air.

Chapter 5

L ove is a red heart. And lust a bright red, sheer g-string. A single trumpet blare. In front of this panty, the brain goes right back to sleep.

Little, low self-inflamed flame. Stamping out that space of itself in high wattage spectacle, shame, and dollar amounts. While taking in the landscape, the eyes put up their hands at the sight, blocking as if to stop the sunlight.

Yes, they meant underwear. Stuff you wear under street or work clothes. Reena thought she could love the challenge and dream-shifting this situation needed. She could not spot Maris right away but could feel her somewhere in this over-populated scene. A fortune in choreographed space. There was a lot of buzz in the air. The bright buzzing of electric light bulbs. Extreme heat from lots of lamps makes brains buzz dizzily. Waves of gossip let loose from the teeth, now buzzing around toothlessly. Canned, musical buzz of scratchy acoustic piano trebly mangled with the viola, courtesy of public radio. Compliments that buzz through kisses and congeal like red-hardened nail polish. Their lips are tapping out a nervous, compulsive buzz-code, flickering under the lights like candied, pornographic radishes. And as they were drifting off to the snack table, they left her alone with…

…emblazoned sky, the sea at sunset – motifs of a middle class bathroom rug or towel. Some dancing sea ferns in alternating deep red and burnt orange, each as tall as a little finger, each made up of just five stalks, bursting open. All arranged in rows and dynamically angled like fireworks across a sky, a joyful pattern. Reining in the gauze and ferns is satiny piping. Merging beneath the crotch, a single satin pipeline, ascending up the back way five inches, fanning out into a quarter-sized sea shell which sits in the small of the back, at the t-bar intersection. Casting the front in blood red hue, investing the sexual organ with the trauma of a wound, then riding up the crevice, this panty wears like a sentence, "To deprive one of one's honor."

Sizing up her not very long and not very slender legs, a complexion that reminded him vaguely of steamed clams, the hair whose color he couldn't think of a name for, the hanging spine, the crooked arms, the photographer waited for an idea to come. He sipped his chai tea and gazed at this bundle of qualities, hoping one of them would suddenly rise up like a green shore to land on. Of course he knows this girl has been hand-picked by Maris who knows exactly what she picks, and has a knack for extracting bodies from cities. "Where's Maris?"

Minute by minute the studio is morphing into an increasingly pathological idea of public space. The noise-level thickens as more people enter. There are lots of young women, lots of their skin. It's a big production. Temperatures rising. Flesh on the stove. People walk in-and-out. This seems disorderly, but it's the noise of production producing good-looking confusion. The stylist puts on a Cat Power CD and, singing along, begins to steam a rack of bras. Recently, on the radio she heard a replay of an old interview with Bob Dylan. When asked if he ever would do commercials, he said… short and semi-toxic… only for women's underwear. Then 2004, it came true, and the song was *I'm Thru with Love*.

The page is a bra for words. It holds a breast-full in place:

Keep separate, support,
elevate, and split the round, spacious
"cheeks" and even keep them from overlapping. Not those "cheeks" with a hole between
them, but those large bulges between the arms. The
cheeks inhabit these spacious apartments. Some are
round, like large potatoes. These that inhabit the hollow
architecture I described are round piles, like humble potatoes,
handsome potatoes. Some of them support the "cheeks" or
"potatoes" I described, and some make them project more, and
some I suspect, lessen them. Many are white their diagonally cut
strips lessen on the sides and ends and they clasp from behind.
A house for these cheeks, a hollow, an architecture, these
structures of beauty are designed with flourishes, fringes, and
ornamentation. Vitruvius probably never could design
apartments like these, separate spacious houses. And
if music, Orpheus could not have fluted such
a musical beauty on his Pandean
pipes. These

flourishes branch off mul-
titudinously. Look how the ornamentation is cast about, before and behind:
flourishes, fringes, fluted and frilled, overlapping
end to end, suggesting trees, towns, houses, with
roofs, clapboards, shingles, and gables. Would I were
there looking in those gable windows beyond those towns
and squares! Of its many styles some others suggest lichens
and mosses. Yet inside these is where life is.

Words cannot properly describe that which is beyond. That
which is under. Yet that which is not visible, that which is squashed
under the architecture, flattened under this bark of this tree, that
which is rejected, hinted at, or held out considerably: what interests me and keeps me interested in life. It never ends until
I'm dead. I like it once or twice removed. I like nothing
on, or maybe I like freedom. I like that house down
there with its fur gables and those pictur-
esque, round piles beyond, over
and upwards.

The stylist's bra-steam is rising.

Maris appeared and kicked things off with one of her classic pep talks, saying this business still had a few sensations lurking in its sleeve if we could all, for once, accept its machine-like nature and not insist on bogging it down with our lazy ideas about art. She was speaking into a bin of underwear, holding up item after item for all to see. Then, while refolding the underwear into neat, little business-card-sized bundles, she confidentially issued encrypted commands to the photographer, "Two words, Bjärne: carcass, automatism. Love, of course, would be a third."

They had Reena run up and down some stairs and then asked her to lie on her stomach on the floor and smoke cigarettes. They massaged a few drops of oil into her hair, combed it out, blow-dried it from various distances, repeating the process several times before smoothing in something that smelled like apricots. Her breasts were lifted by a band of mauve lace. Beside her was an antique ceramic pitcher and porcelain wash basin.

Reena Spaulings as a medieval Russian pilgrim, male. "We'll teach you, you fake saint, not to seduce girls." Two soldiers separating her from a girl who has come to her for help. Reena wearing only underwear.

Reena as Henry David Thoreau with his brother on their boat trip up the Concord and Merrimack rivers. In their tent listening to dogs howling at night. 2nd scene: morning, Reena digging around in the boat for a melon. Brother visible in the tent.

The boy who played Thoreau's brother was named Joey Okorsikens. He and Reena spent a good deal of time in the tent "listening to dogs howling." Joey had beautiful lips. Sandy longish hair, blue eyes, big lips, really a love god, but sloppy looking. A real man? Very stupid? But without a doubt it takes some kind of brains to buck the tide and be simple.

They lay side by side in the tent while Sharon and John came up with something they could both be happy with. Meanwhile,

Joey told Reena the story about the time he did coke in the bathroom of a fancy restaurant with Maris, and how the drugs made her need to shit, which she did right there in front of him because she couldn't hold it. With the giant steak in her belly, three days of constipation under her belt, and cocaine, Maris shitted so into an already-clogged toilet and made it gag with feces and tissue. Overflow. Joey thought they should just leave it but Maris refused to risk anybody thinking it was all hers. True story. So she plunged in with her bare arm, grabbing hold of the turds, hers and the others', pulling them out, breaking them into smaller pieces with her bare hands before dropping them into the toilet again, or some of them temporarily into the garbage. Oh the stench. It made you panic, it elicited roars. Joey was forbidden to leave the bathroom prematurely, so he did more coke. Was Joey lying? Reena looked for signs in his face, but no signs were there. Poor Joey!

Sprawled there in his dark red leather pants, shaking his curls, twitching his eyes, he delivered hot air with a snarly voice right into Reena's ear, jabbing his fingers in the air around her. Was he high? Reena decides to listen to the dogs outside the tent.

They all seem to know each other. There are in-jokes in the air. Also, many different clicking sounds: of computers, of cameras, of lights, speakers, digital impulses, of high heels and wooden slippers. Everybody is talking to somebody, incessantly. Everybody is doing a job. Reena is doing a job. The photographer is nervous. It is a big job. No, it's not... it's not a job, somehow everyone feels it is their own, and that it will move them all wherever they might go, an aesthetic quantum empire.

Dressed, undressed, dressed again. New flesh, new mind, new people.

Her bottom looks like soft white cheese. Mascarpone, spread. A smooth fresh ball. It starts to perspire. She kneels on a wooden crate among scattered bales of hay. The set is rustic, with Italian peasants, goats and wheels of ripening cheese. Her feet are dirty as if dragged across a barn floor. She is posing like a bored, lazy, blank cat. In the sun. It makes no sense. She laughs compulsively.

Reena, as pilgrim again, installed in an empty bathhouse. Legs paralyzed and weak as bits of straw. "With this liquid, I rubbed my legs five times a day. And what happened?"

Maris in the middle of the injunction zone called photo shoot. A look of outer-body detachment, yet she can feel the smells of fears, excitement, existence. She wears black cotton panties most of the time. Every day, though, the ritual requires some change. Perforated. Silky. Smooth. Ribbed. She looks at Reena. That's not only a girl, that's culture.

They fuss with the panties, tucking the flimsy material up into Reena's ass crack and then slowly pulling it out again. They are starting to get into a groove now, and don't need to explain everything as much. The gloomy, this-was-all-a-big-mistake feeling of the morning is suddenly giving way to a manic, grasping-at-mirage-like-breakthroughs feeling. Maris keeps punching the photographer in the back and telling him Reena is not a bowl of fruit. He is like a cautious rabbit being lured out of his hole, starting to sniff around. He smokes a joint on the roof and comes back with ideas. They converse through nods, glances and improvised hand signals, sometimes breaking the silence with a word: "slumpy" "crass" "idiot" "rad."

Reena stands in her museum guard pose, facing the camera and then the wall. They expose 50 rolls in three hours. They take Polaroids between set-ups and have excited conferences around each one, like generals around a battle plan, pushing on, like people who believe they are getting things done, pushing on. Maris is rigid with concentration and sometimes snaps at the studio hands. Maris is glowing with creative purpose and sometimes ecstatically squeezes Reena's hand. In a moment of inspiration that nobody sees coming, she elbows the makeup artist out of the way and begins to draw on Reena's face with a red ballpoint pen.

There is this "I want whatever happens" body and a "nothing ever happens" face and the camera keeps clicking at that face and that face clicks back. It is a brand new camera with an extremely fast motor to capture the moments between the clicks. But there are only voids between the clicks. Deepening the voids, that's what this odd model is doing. The spiritual and the popular are having a meeting, to stretch some horizon? "You will be like the bum on the subway if you don't obey." Where is the soundtrack for that? A couple of girls with clipboards and pencils are arguing in front of the new boom box. It seems the CD player is giving up with nasty gasps of noise. Suddenly everybody is pulling pills or gum or cigarettes or cell phones out of their pockets and handbags. Reena by now looks like a piece of scrap paper with a drawing of a red ballpoint tattoo. Suddenly everybody needs a break and a gallon of water.

(the underwear shoot continues after the break…)

Ok. We need to get her in a bra that's gauzy and pink. We need it one cup size too big for her – that shouldn't be difficult, she's wonderfully flat – so that her breast curls a bit inside it. Then we can see a better nipple. We don't want pointy. We want the breast that ducks down a little and then has a sweet little upturn, makes a J… Reena, put your weight on your right elbow, here, and your cheek against the pillow, shut your eyes, and then point the breast as a capital letter J up into the air.

Now I want light coming in on her from over here, in a stream like a sun ray. I want the sun ray to come down around the breast into the back here between the cushion and spread out and make it look like it's sort of fucking her nipple. Sorry, no offence, but I want to see the light fucking her in this underwear, its technologically innovative fabric, interlocking cotton, and I want to get the light in a stream of metal sun, yes, like that, with a platin filter on the pink.

No, not the pump. Wet them. Bobby get the Evian. Spritz it. Just it, not product. I mean just where it is and the product. And dab. Okay, re-aim the strobe. This has to feel real. Feel bad, whatever. I don't care. It was so perfect for one second and then we lost it. Did we get it? Yes or no.

Lips. Nipple. Nipple. Book. All happening. Just a fog, and the light, and the hair is okay. Are you looking? Shoot before it turns to shit. Do you have to shit? You look like you have to shit.

A brown crown in the lace. It's rising in the light and starting to happen. There. The stuff is lifting, lights up beneath the tip. Wherever you are in your head right now is really working. It has a face. It's in its window. Looking out. It has a brown crown. Tips its hat. It doesn't even know what it is. It's a point and everything starts and ends on it, even the hair, even the logo, even your thoughts. All lined up and all arguments stopped. Anything else to say? I don't know.

(but there is more…)

The nipple should look shocked. As if we just ripped its shirt away, stuck our camera in its face and photographed it. It should look a bit gawky, a pillar of modesty, to heighten the sense of its violation.

Or it should look like it's never known a shirt before, as sun- and air-kissed as possible. Holding its nose up, it is poised, coquette, public. It has as many expressions as the face, having lived as openly and frankly, never having known concealment. It is a person in its own right. With its own personality.

Why are some nipples plump? Plump nipples make breasts more breast-like. When the nipples are small and flat, the breasts are more like shoulders or like… just more stomach. Plump nipples are as good as another set of breasts. Anything pointy or perky implies a hand or mouth to stem its flow.

Today a hot woman is just long legs and pointy nipples. A hot Rembrandt woman on the other hand was a human flesh monster. Pound upon pound of dimpled flesh. She was cloud-shaped. No straight line about her. A shape made up of semi-circles.

Maris says we are all geniuses. She massages Reena's rubbery shoulders with long, cool fingers, then inches the waistband of the panties down a couple of centimeters, exposing their pinkish imprint. The photographer exposes his final roll.

Afterwards John thanked Reena for having integrity, and said he hoped she would be able to continue with it, but Reena said it wasn't integrity because she wasn't whole, she was in pieces. And John said well perhaps you'll be able to remain in pieces, and not become whole. Reena said if I cared about it, I would be whole and not in pieces.

She really did resemble herself exactly. But it wasn't her her. This was illuminated and raw, something hatched in the desert, under a thoughtless sun. Now imagine an unbalanced sun, without filtering, color temperatures way, way off. An international nightmare at noontime. Out-of-control energy, attacking the eyes with laughing immediacy. It was like a freshly dead thing lying on the side of the highway. Her tits hung there in the bra. Her mouth hung there. Her eyes stared out and past her, you, everybody.

From within the core of the breast, in the firm glandular tissue, there is the oblivion of an unreachable consciousness, the impossibility of its knowing how it affects things. Appearances are deceiving, judging by the pinkish-brown radiative zone of the areola, where there seems to be a language of response to anything from words to particles of dust to suction. This much can be said, however: the nipple is stimulated, the muscle fibers will contract, the areola will pucker, and the nipple becomes hard. In any case, as with the sun, the best advice is not to look directly at it at all. There is rarely anything interesting to see anyway. It is much better to let a camera look at it instead.

A beam of waning nipplelight shoots into the inner chambers of the heart, making it recoil and skip in terror, because the heart knows that when the nipple becomes an agent of the sun, everything else is over.

Chapter 6

I t swerved back and forth moving Northeast in jangled spasms.
There was a chance it was going to miss Manhattan and go
straight off the coast, but it didn't.

This is good. I feel like throwing up. Bumpy life. It's the best
I've ever felt. I'm in the air, a tornado. Supersonic. Green flanks of
Jersey wide open. I want them, but not to have them. Just to want
them. I'm a country girl. There's green and blue and brown that
I mix with a thick beige. There's Monmouth County. Close in
and crush. Flanks of Hightown, Princeton, Trenton wide open.
Middlesex County, Beach Haven, I don't even pay attention. I want
to drown. I like it. I like it so much. Don't wait around. Don't pay
attention to the skies either. This is fate. Like the place names,
Arthur Kill Hills, Fresh Kill, Tottenville. What made me happen?
It's the movement. It's what I am, with my one hole! Churn up the
Hudson sparing Hoboken, Weehawken. For that second, there is
no end to that second in a second. It'll be over now soon. My ass!
Fuck you! Ohh! Fuck you!! I don't know where it all started. I was
ready and then something went up me and something went down
me. I was tossed around before I knew what I was doing. People
look at me, but they never read me in my organs. Let's see now,
under the desk, out the window, on a kitchen stool, some shoes.
Once I was just a storm, contemplating my situation. This is just a
small pause. Just a tiny break. It's coming on now. Oh God. Fully

on. Yes, God. Up to 9th Avenue, 8th Avenue. 34th, 48th, high as a plane, goddamn. Landing hard for a few seconds, near Central Park. Yeah. Flush it out. See people. Bones. Clones. Crash into Harlem. Bruised, lit by Times Square. Shattering bulbs. I fall and rise. I whirl and whirl. Nobody will ever see me again here. All this is great. All I ever wanted. Being mud, not carried by a spine. But then I really don't care. This will go on for a while I hope. It is unbelievable how much there is! Such a high rising! Oh, you bastard! I feel like shit! This will change a lot of things. This is changing my life. I'm broken and happy. My life, my rules. I'm the glory of not being here anymore. I'm dust and glorious jelly, with problems. I'm worried. I'm becoming an addict. I care. Downtown to Queens to the Van Wyck via Far Rockaway…

Male models today, you gotta love them. Hard like nails and cute to boot. Lots of hormones just bubbling away, percolating, with cash to spare for beer and weed. The boys at Schlappy, Inc., New York's premiere male modeling referral service, had their shirts off and were body slamming and grabbing each other in headlocks when the squall hit. They were taking turns punching one skinny white arm, trying to make a purple Africa appear there in well-aimed bruises. Schlappy has a receptionist, booker, accountant, and high-speed internet connection, centrally located in Times Square. Four floors up from the office is the "model apartment" that is used for guys who only come to the city for the major castings and pageants.

It's important to be global; you have to give all the dudes a shot. Dudes from Argentina, dudes from France, dudes from Hessen, dudes from La Mancha, dudes from Tyrol, there's lots of dudes to go around.

"Take that, Pony Boy!"

"Hey, why'd you do that? And I liked your look…"

Slick boys in Hawaiian shirts, khaki shorts, and fluorescent sneakers. Decked out in glowing white suits, thronged around, talking and gesticulating rapper-style.

"Ah-ight, shorty. I'll see you tonight." He clicks off his cell phone.

"Yo I'm tired of just looking good. I got to make a name for myself, even if it's graffiti on the street."

"We're the new shit, we're it," says one, perched on top of an overturned dresser, smiling slightly behind mirrored sunglasses. "The old shit is over. Why should we buy somebody else's shit when we can make our own shit and sell it ourselves? We gotta hit all the markets – fashion, music, entertainment, hip-hop, graffiti – the realness of everything. We'll be like, 'This dude is better than that dude,' and that's the truth, and they'll believe it – we'll basically change everybody's opinion for the rest of their life."

"Are you down with us?"

"You know," he adds, "it's like the Rolling Stones song, I can't..." He can't remember the words for a second. "I can't get no satisfaction. I'm never satisfied."

"It's all about being yourself," he says with a shrug.

"We're having mad fun."

"Once I open up my own club, I'll go to it every night and just chill."

"We need some more girl shit," says one.

"Dude, you got the weed?"

"Hmmmm, girls don't come out hard enough these days. Like, 'Yo, what the deal, bitch, what?'"

"I've had the dopest girls, the nicest girls, the prettiest girls," he says breezily. "I've had more girls than all those famous people."

"When I blow up," he's saying, throwing a hand out like a rapper, "I'll shit on everyone–"

A beer bottle is sent rolling, and as he turns to snatch it up again he sees the city disappearing.

"This is dope," he says, smiling.

Now the Empire State Building is gone, blotted out like the rest of New York by a throbbing grey skin. It is thick and low, pressing down and forward – a mean, dark face. Clouds are coming in fast, pushed by super-winds and piling up in the view. The window flexes. The view warps and threatens to snap.

"Ill," he says, still smiling, shaking his head. "Ill."

Then the tornado appeared, creeping in from the left. A dozen guys were gaping. They quit wrestling but they didn't put their shirts on. They sat in leather couches, or stood in their socks with open mouths suddenly interrupted by the howling and the darkness. The TV was out, but not the lights. The CD was still turning, but couldn't be heard with the howling wind. So they microwaved some popcorn and consoled each other with slaps on the ass, getting it up the ass jokes and surprise head butts. There was still plenty of beer left. The boys hunkered down and watched everything from their place on the 19th floor.

It came at them like a movie. A dark funnel, wide at the top, pointy at the bottom, and twisting in the middle. It moved with a slow rage you could feel in every part of you. It was better than digital dinosaurs – much, much better looking than a giant enraged ape or refried nuclear mega-iguana. It looked bigger than the buildings, way more impressive. Was there any way to stop it? It inspired giddy, child-like terror. Its nasty swirling was breathtaking and stomach-turning. It was a living thing, thrusting its super-life on the rest of life and sucking it all up into itself. What was kind of funny was the chaos of it. It was funny just to see it there, but also the thought of how it sucked, how it trashed everything like a brawling bum and made the people run away screaming, if they could get away without getting sucked into it too. It reminded them a little of whatever they've watched before: an evil black vagina thing that comes whenever somebody touches a ring; an ominous knee-slapping dance performed by homicidal Bavarian hicks; zombies that bite chunks of flesh from their girlfriends and parents; horrible contorted things that rip out of the stomach, eat their way out of the asshole, or burst forth from every blood vessel. It was definitely scary too, scarier than all that and so crazy because it was real – the realness of everything. It was willing to go there. To escalate. To disrespect. It was the realest.

They saw windows sucked from the sides of office buildings and into the vortex, which was full of other things too, a clattering, churning, groaning junk pile. They burst into cheers and danced. It moved through the city like a mad saw. It blackened with the things that disappeared into it. It was speckled. Expert valet parking: a car was lifted up and moved several blocks by it. Angry busboy: it snatched up all the food, tables and chairs of a sidewalk café. Were those people? Maybe. They could be people or things. Nouns. It was hard to see the details but you could hear everything inside of it as it got closer.

A couple of the boys tied themselves together with a bathrobe sash and huddled in the corner, then used an extension cord to fasten their sashed bodies to a 200 pound set of barbells. Another hid under the bed. The rest backed up to the far wall and sat on the floor, hugging their knees and watching, stoned and mesmerized by this high-production catastrophe out the window. It was too loud to hear what anybody was saying. Were they even talking? Familiar faces twisted into expressions of stoned panic, ecstatic ending, shit in pants, scared delight, and pinch me this isn't happening. One guy was crying, either from fear or from fear plus joy. What was he thinking? These feelings were strange to see. They were beamed into these lanky, glossy bodies by the wind and the roar, transmitted into them by the view.

The sky was thickening. Blowing dust and dirt. If you dropped a postcard of New York City into a blender with dust, dirt and water and put it on "high"... and then dimmed the lights...

The thing was approaching and picking up speed. A boy ran to the bathroom and bolted himself in. The others stayed put, nailed to the floor. Here it comes, here it comes. They were watching with their entire souls, and their eyes were clear little soul windows now. Glassy windows opened directly on the horror and the beauty of it as it got blacker and faster. It was awesome, and the scarier it got the funnier it looked. You could see faces laughing but with the sound of the tornado instead of laughing. Were they tripping?

Strange beams were aimed at it now, some kind of yellow emergency lights. Lights never seen before. Like an Olympic figure skater, the tornado danced in and out of them as they tried to track it, spotlighting its dark coils for a few seconds at a time. This was the most beautiful part.

The window popped. Everything loose, like shirts and bottles, was sucked out in one sudden breath. A tree flew by. A blur of objects. And that was definitely a person.

Several seconds of just rushing, fast-forwarding blurs of grey, black, grey, black. It was becoming an experimental film. It was sped up fog, but a fog full of teeth that made a ton of noise. The building was swaying back and forth and groaning deep inside. Someone vomited into his own lap. Another thought he heard words coming out if it like it was talking to itself:

"I always wondered how does thought diminish… Well, for one, people get cracked and lashed by an almost constant state of tears. We become of this world. Oddly this makes us more odd, as the world is odd. The earth is odd, der erde, with two d's three e's and two r's. My love made the mistake (again) of going private. This novel will not make that mistake because it is unable to. Do you know how they wrote it? They were never alone, solitary. The authors of this novel were heroes. This novel will sit beautifully like a piece of red cake on a plate, wanting you but not wanting to do anything to you."

It was backing off now, inching menacingly away. Eardrums popped and lungs compressed. The atmosphere squeezed you like a fist, harder and harder, and then gradually relaxed. And then you could breathe again.

We should keep on going, out as far as the Rockies, tunneling in and popping out again like a head, throwing boulders down either side. Ten million dune buggies sweep in from the plains, carrying a flood of nude hippie ghosts with rifles and hatchets. Show us a riot, folks, and we'll tell you about a tornado. On the first day, as the murderous wave was advancing, bells were ringing all over town, and people were fleeing. Whether it was a question of a mob or a monster mattered little, the effects were the same: corpses, heaps of corpses made by other corpses. The houses were almost deserted, the owners evacuated, only a few servants left ironing and folding the linen, ironing and folding in a panic.

A riot and a tornado can both be absorbed into the category of annual disasters, which is to say that they only become events tallied onto a greater ledger, a wider story. On the news they said not to leave your house until further instructions and to call any friends or relatives who might be unaware. I looked out my window and the streets were completely empty. Usually it's crowded on my block. Then at midnight everyone in my building went down to the basement. We all sat around on the floor. I talked to a couple of people I had never talked to before. When it came it was like hundreds of subways passing at once. At one time it got so loud we felt the vibrations of the walls. Our building is pretty new and it didn't get hurt too badly. When I went upstairs this morning the TV's were out. But after a couple of hours channel 2 was back and they actually had a video of a person being lifted up. They said that the updraft in a tornado can be up to 200 miles per hour. It looked fake the way he was carried. Like in an old trick animation. I haven't gone outside yet even though they say it's safe. They showed Times Square on the news. All of those crazy signs were smashed on the ground or the glass was broken. Cars were lifted up and smashed into the sides of buildings. Almost all of the street signs and street lights were knocked over. Trees in Central Park were torn out of the ground. Rooftops were covered with dead pigeons. Wall Street was interrupted. They said it isn't clear yet how many people were killed.

Reena slept. In the night, in the howling storm. She is closed eyes, open mouth, saliva gathering in the corners. She is on her back with legs 40 degrees apart. Like a swimmer. The occasional swallow, the frequent, measured and unconscious breaths. Indistinct murmurs, maybe a sequence of numbers, maybe random. Her sheets flap and snap in the wind through the open window, and one hand clutches them to her breast. Like water. The other hand is cast up over the unconscious head, sleeping there in the pillow hills. She dreams about sailing.

This book is also for the boys, who could still feel the building moving. It sits with them now, but later will walk in their back pockets, flexing against their slim asses like the flexing window they were watching the tornado from, as happy to be in its place as it is ready to break. They read it out loud to each other in line at the bank or at a casting call. Before it's over it will contain ships on fire, communism, Karl Lagerfeld, money, cancer and zombie-cowboys. The kids have survived the tornado like they've survived everything so far, and the book goes safely with them. Where to next? We move through a city that produces boys and girls and extends itself through them. Our freedom of movement, which we insist upon as we move through this these dry lake bed times, is a kind of writing too. Swaying on slim hips, striding on thin legs, rolling its narrow shoulders, head loose on its neck, the novel moves in them and they move it. Note: get more old people in here too. And some body fat. We love you.

Chapter 7

I think, get up idiot!

I think about the red numbers spelled on the alarm clock.
I think about getting up.

I think, let me have a look at my face, did anything horrific take place in the night, like in a science fiction film, which I always secretly expect?

I think, let me relieve myself. I think about the dust that gathers so quickly on the white tiled floor, and the shower hairs left high and dry by receding waters. A cult has arisen. Without proper arguments or any established philosophy, but with an aesthetic as tough as weeds, which is significant to kitsch.

I think this is the weirdest time of my life. It feels like being showered with 100 roses. Or just sniffing life. Even not giving a damn about flowers, I think it all happened so fast and came as a surprise. I think about the pee-toilet bowl acoustics and about the cotton rectangle on the inside of my underwear. Perhaps it will make me strong. I give all, will not receive anything. I think, take three squares of toilet paper, fold first along the perforations and then fold the whole thing in half. Every three seconds I'm fine. Every second second I give up. Every five seconds I rise up. Feeling perpetually x-ed.

I think naked before the mirror. I think about how I look from the front, with shoulders proper and back, and then with shoulders slouched, like normal. I think about my body – is it sexy? Or better, is it touching? Could a man be moved by it? I think, do I have any cellulite and are my breasts holding up their youthful shape? I think about my shoulder muscles, which all on their own decide from day to day if they will appear masculine or somewhat feminine, the different shades of my body, the relative white of my thighs, my ass, my stomach, the darker shade of my shins, arms and back, the splotchier bothered skin of my face, hands and feet. This is a banality but it should be better understood.

I think about the crack in the 11 inch all-in-one TV/VCR and about the throw rug from Bed, Bath & Beyond. I think about the nook of bad spirits, the crevice between my dresser and some stackable plastic storage units, which I have unconsciously made into the bad energy ghetto, the bad part of town of my room where I put soiled rags, my liquor bottles (both empty and full), my cigarettes and ashtrays (when I am trying to quit), plastic bags, and whatever else I prefer to hide from myself. I think about my nails and the receding pools of gold nail polish. I think about the dust on the CD player, the week-old flowers, the faux wood paneling of my desk top, as I crack my back to the left and then the right and do some neck rolls. I think, while inspecting my feet, with so much city around us our bodies are all we have to become dazzled by nature's unmanufactured forms, growths, cracks, fractures, fissures, deformities and transformations. I think about my black plastic wastepaper basket to my left, which I peed in one night when I was too lazy to make it to the bathroom. I think, I like the floor a lot, as I go lie on a piece of it and look up out of the window, thinking of how the sky is shoved to the periphery of the stage by our monuments and monumental buildings.

I think as I tap on my computer,

Dear _____,

Everything's fine with me. Now that it's almost spring, each day around 4 o'clock, I speed down to the water to read for an hour or two. It's almost time to take out those sunglasses I bought from Daffy's last fall. Yesterday, as I approached the water, I discovered a movie was being shot. The scene was about a man drowning in the East River. It was great fun for us onlookers to watch a man dramatically drowning and in grave danger.

Lots of love,

R

I think, my chin in the hole of my coffee mug, about:

Sun hats

I would like to buy a sun hat, and also by the way, a large green frog hair clip like the one I saw the other day on a small girl.

I have turned the various possibilities around in my head and have so far ruled out baseball caps, cowboy hats, visors, church hats and straw hats.

The desire for a sun hat builds in me each day. I know I will get one. And that now it is only a question of one of these days, sooner or later, happening upon (without even looking for it) the one I know is predestined for me. My spiritual mate as sun hats go.

This is how I go about treating whatever I might need in life, be it a sun hat, a job, or an operation. I recognize the need or desire and then I go about my affairs. Letting the forces of the universe that deal with these matters, bring the thing and me together. I believe that there is a supernatural power, although I cannot prove it, that will guide whatever you want to you, and say, "Here!" People worry so much about satisfying each and every one of their consumer impulses immediately, going on day-long, city-wide outings for them. If they only knew!

The Urban Boulevard

You are on your way. The boulevard is crowded. It is a busy avenue after all. The people move purposefully. Briskly. Men upright, making efficient strides. Some strollers. Tourists. Shoppers. Pedestrians annoy other pedestrians. As if no one can believe that other pedestrians exist and might crowd them or get in their way. A thoroughfare is all. A route of circulation. Like an aqueduct, or a badger's underground tunnels, or the migration of birds. But it's not graceful like a bird's flight. Nor rurally charming like a badger's tunnels.

Maybe like a horse race where the horse is whipped to gallop as fast as he can. Trying to overtake the one next to him. Clip. When people become pedestrians they are like cars. Their movements dart strategically, they roll fast. Pedestrians and automobiles are the same. Stop and go. For cars it's the effect of traffic lights. For pedestrians it's the same as well as the products, words and other signs that continuously crowd their attention, all the way down the boulevard. Stores are like little havens from the stressful thoroughfare. Restaurants are gas stations for people. Bars and bedrooms are our garages. I come home and park. I idle for a while, then turn off the ignition.

Beds

Beds are always nice to lie down in. I like the feeling of my skin on the worn cotton sheet. I like it. I like to feel it against my cheek, under my palms, and to rub the soles of my feet on it. There's nothing like turning in bed, feeling the softness anew, switching to another blessed position. It's always nice to sleep late, right through those morning hours. To sleep at night is necessary, but during those golden sunshine-filled hours it is luxurious.

I think I'll play with my hair. Why not? Why not. I think I'll sit down. I think I'll put on a wrap, I'm a little chilly. I know I'm lost. I think, I have to pee again and about the sun breaking into the apartment by each window. Why is it I'm so what is not open? I think about the gray painted wood floors as I drag the R2D2-esque vacuum cleaner about the apartment.

I think, dear artists (even those whom I like), you can't escape it, you are making art that approximates life and I'd prefer, at the very least, life that approximates life. I think how my body is my brains and how my brain doesn't have a brain.

I think I wanna throw up. Why is this world cluttered with female matter? Showing the goods, the skin, the legs, armpits. I'm sick of it all. The wispy chic waifs, the wannabees, the sneaky smiley one, the cold-fingered, the smelly, diva-esque one the bright one the stomping wild one. Never was there such an exposure to the business of beauty. Thrown into a kind of confusion. You love them all. You hate them all. All the time. Enjoying it. Why not?

I think to be stabbed or bloodily beaten would somehow be like a vacation from this. I think how neurotic I am that my cigarette has to find the precise center of my lips before I will drag on it. I think about life at sea, a writer named Jousse, and how time flows both forwards and backwards. I think, something about the citizen's life – the limits and matter of it – makes me stand apart always considering it, entertaining the feasibility of life within it but, no matter from what angle I look at it, no matter all the activity and smiles and colors emanating from it, no matter how long I stare at it, I can't go in. So I skirt the perimeters of it, like I did the other day with Central Park, sticking to Fifth Avenue but eyeing it the whole way down. I think how can we make a beautiful brushstroke with our existence?

Maris thinks I'm hot stuff. At least for now. She is so on all the time. She wants that high known as success, she is a hardcore addict, and I'm her stuff. And I like to be her stuff right now. I make her so happy she could kiss the world. I think when happy she is the best party in town, a walking party. She is vulgar, frank, naked, visual. A fully decked out operator, power-perfect. I think she thinks she fucks with my head and makes me do things. Perhaps one day I'm gonna kill Maris, no, holy shit that would be stupid, more likely become her lover and then kill her.

Holy shit, how often I imagine murdering the ones I love. And them murdering me. Do people do this to me too, in their minds? Why is it that we all don't go around with guns, like Mexicans in a Peckinpah film? Imagine that. I just think we shoot each other differently now. With cameras, for example. A shift of attention is like throwing a bomb. I love you and I hate you are little bombs.

Holy shit, Maris was downstairs. Why is it that Reena jumped into some tights and a t-shirt, splashed some cold water on her face and buzzed her in? I just think that nobody could have been more manic and effective than Maris Parings. She was a production machine of today, a think tank in ticking heels. Wielding her yoga-toned arm, reaching in. So it happens: Maris shows up. So this is your place.

Maris had installed herself as a sort of dial by which the patterns and rhythms of Reena's life were suddenly being tweaked and adjusted. For reasons of her own, Maris took an interest in arranging situations in which Reena would be revealed or take on value and illusory new motion. There was the business side of it, but there was more. Maris eyed Reena. She put her face close to Reena's and breathed her in like smoke. Reena had no idea what Maris was really up to but something in her was definitely responding. Like a quarterback in the field, she was tuning in to the woman's urgent, coded play calling, and her zen, invisible to the viewing audience and to the opposing team. Maris was pacing the sidelines with her clipboard face. Reena was out there with her radio helmet.

Neither of them spoke of the tornado. Maris was leaning against the kitchen wall, staring at some snapshots of a summer vacation Reena had taken with her ex-boyfriend and some other friends last year. Her eyes took in the views of bodies and sand, the sunburned boredom of these moments, trying to decipher something there. Somebody had scribbled all over the photos with a Sharpie, x-ing out eyeballs and adding cryptic thought bubbles over the heads. "Cape Cod?" Reena nodded.

Reena put on some coffee. The gasket was worn out and the thing wailed like a wounded animal as it began to percolate. The Hasidic neighbors' six children were making ceiling-thunder from above with what sounded to Maris like wooden shoes, if not hooves. Maris sniffed at her armpits, confessing that she hadn't bathed in days. Reena tried to amuse her by doing cartwheels and juggling grapefruits. The rain finally stopped.

There was so much to do in New York if you felt compelled to and Maris seemed to have reasons for being everywhere all the time. Reena agreed to show up here and there, Thursday, Saturday, etc, and even gave Maris permission to include her in a casting for the first film of a big, but overblown and uninteresting 90s artist who had some collector-friends in Hollywood. Half-listening, Reena found herself contemplating Maris's perfect, pointy little breasts. They were so elegant and sharp-looking, hard little sea shells under her tasteful top. Her teeth were a string of small, even pearls. Everything about her was honed, toned, and polished smooth as sea stones. But she smelled funny today, fishy, or was that the kitchen trash? They sucked on cigarettes and listened to the stopped rain. Maris finally rose up on her heels and handed Reena a check for $10,000. "You were great, Reena, really perfect."

As soon as Maris had left, Reena waited exactly five minutes, then ran to the bank and deposited her money. The sun was out. Money, money, money. She was already making a shopping list in her head. Oil paints, the best quality and all the colors. She would rent an art studio in Brooklyn. Call her drug dealer. Fill her bathroom with nice things. Shoes. A palm tree. A plane ticket to Paris or a used car, a Volvo like Ro's, an Escalade, even. Walking out of the bank she realized that all she really wanted was a hamburger and maybe a beer. No. She started to puke, mentally, even thinking about establishing this kind of peace in her life. She had an inbuilt convulsive system that went into alarming modes, a hard and spastic heart was placed in her breast. She would blow her wage as quickly as possible… if you could only blast cash out of a cannon, the ultimate spending machine.

Holy shit a little money alright. I just think I might have gotten a little more of it though. Why is it that when you do so little for it, no amount of recompense is enough. Holy shit this is six months' worth of standing guard at the Met. I just think that when you're serving time for it, a sense of reality allows the dollar amount to remain small and still seem OK, to trickle in at the same pace as the hours do, whereas when you're selling nothing you're selling an essence which is priceless. Why is it that essences are so light? Holy shit it's my economy, an economy of essences. I just think I have a slow leak. Why is it that I can go to bed so warm and wake up so cold for instance. Holy holy holy holy shit.

I think, I will not sink into this stupor. No way. Every day getting up, I will observe more sharply. Will study my options in all detail, and at the exact moment get up on my perfect wave of will. I think a whole ocean full, forever. I feel that force inside me. Why is it that my story starts feeling like the history of a war?

I think I'm a profile of panic. Painting a vase, a book, a bird and 10,000 years of history. Searched and employed. Resistance, existence, resistance, existence. I think I'm going crazy. Finally. Some light shining through holes in my curtain. Why is it? For a while now I've been seeing signs in the subway: "Desire is War" (an ad for a TV dramatization called *Helen of Troy*). All-out war like the Trojan one.

She remembered an older friend having explained to her the buddhist-cockroach-holy-shit existences of the poets. Notably the late Allen Ginsberg quite a bit, admiring his unflinching all-encompassing holy shit attitude. But then these words by Valerie Solanas stuck in her mind: "The shit you have to go through in this world, just to survive." Was Reena a survivor too?

Forcing herself through the clogged Chinese section of Grand Street, she had plenty of time to think about it. She decided that survival was not real life, not what you'd call elaborating a life-form, certainly nothing to be proud of, no matter how glamorous and strong those beautiful bitches in Destiny's Child made it seem. Survival was for concentration camps. Yes, New York was a kind of camp too, an updated, fun version of one, she had to admit it, but she felt she'd rather be gassed than...

Holy shit, an untamed energy. Why is it that it lies and sleeps within us all but never explodes? I just think it's a city of many small fires. The forces of finance attempt to stamp them out by converting them into something else. The lid is on, and...

Holy shit, I gotta light up.

Chapter 8

COMMUNISM

Obviously the first thing I notice about him is his nose. It was
and is the largest nose I have ever seen. In the movie Cyrano
De Bergerac, Gerard Depardieu's nose is long as if someone had
grabbed the tip and pulled it outward, stretching it. But his nose
is not like this. It is more like a mountain. Between the eyes the
ridge of the nose moves away from the face at a slightly downward
angle, running into a knobby bump. The tip of the nose is a square
with rounded edges. It is probably based on his posture as a whole,
but the first words his appearance evokes are "noble nose." A pride
and a confidence (maybe sexual) seems to reside in and exude from
there.

He is working in an old Polish restaurant, wearing a white
apron. He looks Eastern European just based on the shape of his
face. Between the tables and chairs I can't see what he dresses like.
It turns out that he dresses almost exactly as I had imagined and
hoped. He wears narrow, light blue jeans which are a little short so
that they show his white tube socks. His loafers and windbreaker
are of unfamiliar brands to me. He always wears a loose T-shirt,
either black or white, sometimes with a pocket. The surprise was
that his shirts were always blank. I never saw him promote an
organization, school, or movie on a shirt.

As he moves through the restaurant carrying trays and moving
glasses he is in a daze, not self-conscious. I have seen him at the

restaurant many times before I had the courage to speak to him. I wonder how it must feel to know that everyone is noticing one's nose. Later on, when I meet him often for lunch or coffee, I find that he has built up a wall to the stares from strangers. I think he even feels that people are envious of his nose because it's something he possesses that they do not.

He talks slowly and pauses to plan out his English sentences but never stutters. He is probably unaware that his simple statements are so eloquent. He also does not mind sitting in silence with me. He will stare off into space. I enjoyed staring at him because I loved his face and his eyes were beautiful green and hazel receptors.

How can I explain that my feelings for him were deep and genuine even though what I loved most about him was his face and body? He really had a perfect body. He was thin, but not at all skinny. I could only grip my hand a quarter of the way around his bicep and a strong vein ran along the muscle. His fingers were long and thin, but again, not skinny. He looked strong and fit in a way that comes from random manual labor, not from working out. He was 6'2". He was naturally pale but he had a tan from spending a lot of time outside. His skin was just on the border between boyish smoothness and manly leatheriness. He had a hint of the beginning of a crow's foot at the corner of each eye.

He makes love maturely, slowly and solidly. He is subtly sensitive and passionate in his movements but his facial expression is Stoic. Sometimes we make eye contact, sometimes we look past each other, and I feel the muscles in his back with my hands and calves. He seems so serious but I know his mind is full of tenderness. When we have finished he rolls over on to his back with his arms spread out. He pulls me over so that I lay with my head in his pouch, and he falls asleep. Almost always when we awake from our after-sex nap he relates some strange dream that makes little sense.

I wonder at how every customer at the restaurant did not feel overwhelmed with the desire to speak to him. It was sad to see him there in his apron when his body seemed destined for something greater.

I look to him as source and residue of a dream. I somehow don't get tired of him as I do with other men. Not so fast. He is the slow burning man. Perhaps because he is the most complex and the finest recipe for disaster I could sense in a man over a long period of time. He welcomes the inspiration of others. There are plenty of incidents, plenty of desires he ignites in people. Lets them simmer. Then kicks them out. After the slow burn there is a tough fire, and then go play with the ashes. The man with the gray hands. I see lots of shades of browns and grays and other ambiguous colors when I think of him. Then he shoots out of it in the middle of a party, morphing into intense flirts, then moves back into whatever you might sense is himself. Like an odd kind of sea creature. His mind has sensitive and shiny tentacles that he can wrap around anything and anybody. As ingenious as he is massively evasive. Very rarely it happens that he can look somebody straight in the eye. I know quite a few people who have tried. Only when kind of drugged is he able to adjust and focus, but then it's more like a stare. Like a Miles Davis music clip in the sort of decadent-80s *Decoy* era. A few of my female friends have noticed this feature and like me asked themselves why that is. We are still trying to figure it out. Making people love this kind of game is part of his existence and his resistance too. But there have been massive sufferings. He is an homme fatale, but nobody realizes that until having been hit. One cannot be careful enough around him. But then there is a deadpan wit in his artily sloppy clothes, so nondescript they attract all kinds of projections. Most hidden. Most obvious. Intense blandness. It frequently cracks me up. A burst of laughter is like make-up sex with him.

Something flashes in the sun at the other end of the next car. It's a blonde head. A tow-head. A man with a tow head has stepped into the narrow band of sunlight between the platform overhang and the train to snuff out a cigarette. He seems to look around him briefly, possibly in her own direction, then climbs unsteadily back onto the train. She has the impression of baggy clothes: a faded zip-up with a drapey hood and some kind of faux Navajo print, and old pants, like sweatpants and cargo pants at the same time. The shape of a man's hair when he decides to cut off signature long hair but wants to keep the memory of it alive somehow. One identity over and gone, and only a provisional reminder to replace it.

Yes, he must have seen her during the platform recess because a little while later when the train is moving again the tow-headed figure in the baggy clothes lurches to a stop in the aisle next to her seat and asks, "D'you wohnna drink a bur?" He motions vaguely in the direction of the lounge car. The skin is tanned on his forearm. And smooth, like the arm of some beautiful Quaker antique chair or a subtly stained balustrade. She declines with a frosty but friendly "no thank you" that reminds her of her mother and he moves on without her. He doesn't look back. He doesn't even say goodbye.

His face had been strong if bleary, his eyes a piercing and hollow West Virginia blue. Broad brow, hale jaw. Deep vertical creases in the cheeks framing a full mouth. His could have been one of those haunted faces you see in pictographs of Confederate soldiers during the Civil War. Later in the day he shuffles by again, and she sees that his hair has become more stringy.

His clothes say it for him: we're not happy. From the store where they were bought, they're asked to function, to not stand out, and nothing more. They are his second skin: tracing lines from the medicine cabinet in the mornings (for aspirin), to auto-inflicted existential crises in the afternoons, to a heading out into the ecstatic fold of bodies, drinks, and revelry at night. Their motto: hang in there. Jeans are parched and brittle, sweaters are fraying, threads are unraveling. More clothes than body – though he is heartwrenchingly appealing – when he moves the effect is of fabric swooshing and large shoes clomping.

Occasionally he appears before my eyes, the figure in Edward Munch's *The Scream*. His face stamped in existential shock and horror. His hair – which never got treated like hair, that is combed, cared for, or managed – is just an extension of the stage of his face. And it plays a superb supporting role in this expressionistic drama.

I would also add that he is the human counterpart of the street cat – tattered ear, missing tail, matted fur viciously chomped at in several places… A resilient and persevering soul, whose body has been dragged through hostile terrains – his being the dark existential interiors of his own emotions.

(There is public space – a dance floor, a classroom, and there is private space – a home, a bed. And there are more complex inhabitations which rely on being a function of both – like the pervert's dark corner.)

His suspicion that he is a travesty, causes him to throw himself into the populated night – to seek out intense couplings, groupings, endless configurations of experiences – to be out and absorbed into the nocturnal fold of bodies, desires, motion, but at the same time to sublimate his features, his qualities, his presence, so in the end he doesn't project – his emotion and confusion shrouding him. Come evening, he – who is always the same – goes from his home – which is always the same – to be re-absorbed into the ecstatic and ever-changing night.

I often found myself admiring his lower legs and feet. These were the only definitive parts of his body. They announced themselves. His feet were proud of their handsome form, how good they looked in his straightforward shoes, how sure and frank of a base they made. But his lower legs and feet were so nice to look at greatly due to their conjunction with the rest of his body and in that they jutted out of what reminded me of a young deer's legs: they were so long and straight that they gave the impression of a youthful awkwardness, of a still-growing, and of ligaments and knobs. He seemed to have soft skinny thighs, and from there – his ass, torso, shoulders, arms – his body became more that of a mature horse, sexy and shank-like. But if his lower legs and feet were a frank edifice, they were the grounding to a top that was in constant sway – like a tall plant or beanstalk. Up and up, his body became pure emotion, less and less straightforward, more and more confused, shy, conflicted. By the time you got to his head, it was all penduly and bobbing and his hair like a piece of forgotten grass.

It was only when he was indifferent – and he was capable, although it was rare, of a frightening and cold indifference – that everything stopped moving, and what materializes is a most handsome and masculine specimen. Then it would all be set in motion again.

In this city called New York he is attractive to me. He and his friends. These particular life forms. Rummaging through their effects, the things they carry on their persons, in a backpack or a plastic bag, you might find a water bottle filled with vodka. A silly keychain. A peanut butter and jelly sandwich. A strange snapshot. Bulging spiral notebooks. Books. Magazines. Xeroxes of books and magazines. A precious book wrapped in paper towels.

They are like literature come to life, resembling it more than the human. Snoring literatures. Pissing literatures. Bathing literatures. TV watching literatures... Because of their quality of facelessness with their costumes of normalcy and invisibility. Or in that their beings don't state. They are without ideals. They flower rather. There is a subtlety and a poetry, a human appropriation of literatur-ic space and movement... What kind of literature are they? Well, I really am an ignorant person... a Bataillian kind perhaps?

He really is so attractive that I am often overtaken with a physical feeling that when translated into a visual thought, has me hurtling through space in order to get stuck onto him, wherever he might be, the goal being to seal as much of my surface as possible onto his body. The desire for contact is so strong, that it becomes amplified and exaggerated and I imagine skin magnified, and in place of a caressing, a rubbing and scraping.

Stick my nose in it. The rose. All charm dripping from a slightly bowing head. The soft type. Bowing to the ladies. A man of conscious constraint. Everybody and everything is greeted all the time with creamy smooth yet respectful hellos and remarks; the full-on "too charming to be true" vibe. This lasts only and exactly as long as the moment of introductions he seems to master like no other. His picture has been appearing in the gossip columns a lot because of that. But at the end of the day it's all about bonding over beer and pussy with his buddies, who are a zoo-like and grotesque kind of lot. Sometimes he behaves in a truly Howard Sternian way. The fascination here is that I really can't figure out how this can still make him desirable. With shimmering boldness he is getting a maximum out of conventions. He never lets a woman touch his hair. Well there's a spot for magic to happen or a punch in the face.

His body is there, live and available, easily turned on. Simply the way in which, when he sits, his long stretched out legs and eventually one of his feet moving around may interfere in our conversation. But he remains nicely entangled in his thinking as this is not contradictory and he knows it. His body and the head that's on top of it are there and willing to turn you on as well, and you can accept and enjoy this as simply as it comes. So you keep on talking.

Nothing in particular to declare about his style – rather insignificant – or about his face – it is pleasant – nor about his body. But he does have a little bit of a belly – a sexy belly he's more or less decided to afford and which consequently he's trying to capitalize on. It could be read as the surfacing of some sort of generosity, as you'd put it speaking of a girl's features. Whatever, he knows how to carry it along with the rest of his sharp thirty-something years of age, hence a persuasive and fulfilling physicality, hanging out with him, side by side, and ultimately too before, when, and after we fuck. Something you grow addicted to, something you miss soon after. No gap between the bodies, simply the necessary distance between two pairs of eyes, just to be able to focus sometimes.

You read in his look: he's shameless of being in demand and of taking on that position, so it becomes the opposite of a self-indulging vulnerability. Were it not for his delicately lazy eye-lids, working as some kind of censoring but nevertheless sensual shades, you'd just be eaten up by his see-through glances. And, in turn, never have eyes been so connected to mouth, to his own and to the other's, or to anyone else's – that's the beauty of it. Wouldn't it be silly to resist the inclusive desire emanating from his person? A potential aspiration to fuck the entire planet, as a consumer indeed, but also just as a way to communicate desire itself.

I still get all wet when I see him after all these years. He hasn't changed a bit, still wears that ethnic ropebelt, doesn't matter if it's with a suit or sweatpants, the knitted Tibetan, deadhead whatever you call that dirty little piece of fabric so tight around his waist. He's always been slightly bloated and pasty skinned, almost always has 3" sweatcircles under his arms and on the back of his ass. His hair is medium brown and slightly shorter than you know he'd like it ideally, and he always shaves his sideburns totally off. There's something so hot about those little smoothly shaven pale areas, diagonally above his attached earlobes, especially when a tiny drip of sweat slowly trickles down… reminds me of the porcelain smooth and soft skin I find when I shave my bikini line on those long hung-over Sundays when I'm bored and just play with myself and stare at the beige wallpaper all day in my dark, dirty little room. In high school he used to smoke pot and hang out with the deadheads, but whenever they put their new bootleg cassettes on from the Greek Theatre '86 or Saratoga '87, he'd get this intense look in his eyes and stare way out into space because he had only one passion in the world – this other, old Manchester postpunk guitar band The Chameleons UK – he was SO into them and everyone he knew knew it. That band was all his in our small town in Southcentral Virginia.

I used to see him in the parking lot smoking cigarettes in his white Jetta with the tan interior before school with his head down, hands on the steering wheel fiercely concentrating on the charismatic boooming icy echoes of the lead singer's voice who he always just called "marky." Then he'd open the car door to decompress, put on his baggy jean jacket with the crying mimeface rainbow iron-on patch from the Chameleons' rare 1st album. I always pictured him rolling off me all sweaty after frenetically pummeling me with the short thick rockhard cock I always pictured was restrained by that soiled ropebelt. I'd stop him for a second to flip him over and slide him into my mouth, taking him down my throat and running my tongue over the red marks the strangling ropebelt always I'm sure makes on his soft hips… as I'm sucking him I can't stop thinking of how important The Chameleons are to him, and what if Marky died, and how no one feels for them the way he does…

He was the one she ended up sitting next to at a dinner in honor of her friend's 25th birthday. Interrupting her impassioned declaration that war sucks, he had calmly passed her a tray of beans and said, "Anyway, there's no point in discussing such things if we can't find a way of talking about them that's as outrageous as the things themselves." That's when a smiling, winking slightly scary void opened up between them. She blushed and felt suddenly too drunk to make it on foot to the bathroom.

"The dandy," wrote the English belle-lettrist Cyril Connoly, "is but the larval form of a bore." Thomas Carlyle pointed to a world of work in need of being done, and then to the dandy, "a Clothes-wearing Man, a Man whose trade, office and existence consists in the wearing of Clothes." Beau Brummel designed himself as a "visual object" to assert the irreducible and inalienable intractability of selfhood. The visual object called an abstract painting does the same on behalf of its maker's self, opening a blank space in the texture of institutionally recognized meaning. Few artists leave that void empty for long.

Small hands, almost like a girl. Paleness. Set against black clothes. Always. There is one set for work and one set to go into the streets with. He doesn't leave his cave-like garage very much. To take a ride on the motorcycle. Or get something to eat. He walks very upright, tight ass, dark voice that sounds always bigger than his body. The voice and the body don't really relate. There is a bare-boned economy in his life. That's it. Lived minimalism. Makeshift meals. Tough passions. No mistake about his hands. When his body and brain are jolted, they can beat the shit out of somebody or something. They are small, but can be very angry. He might use some metal ring to knock out the enemy. Not only provocation but also attraction can move him to the point of violence, and he turns all that into hardcore art, comical fury, presented through a kind of gutted minimalism. His is the most profound form of refusal since it is in no way the assertion of the opposite principle. I adore his economy and subsequent autonomy. I wondered about how he looks like with no clothes on at all.

I remember the first time I saw him very well. He was walking down from the promontory to the lake. It was a typical Swiss summer day, the sky was a lightly bleached tint of blue, and the rocks must have been burning the sole of his feet as he made his way down to the water.

He walked with the confidence of those men who know themselves to be attractive to women and homosexuals alike, and there was something slightly unnerving about it. Every step seemed to be communicating a masculinity that was both aware of itself as an object of desire and as a projective force. The careful balance of his step, the way it seemed absolutely unhindered from its course by the burning prick of the rocks, his poise was instantly bothersome to me. I thought: look at the pretty, broad and straight shoulders, look at the eyes as clean as the still water of the lake around them, look at the hips moving with the faintest reminiscence of a sway. From so many Italian movies at the Cinemathèque he had learned the romance of the Mediterranean, yet everything I saw spelt out Lake Geneva and not the Adriatic.

When he reached the waterfront, he laid his towel out on the pebbles, pulled out a book from his bag, and started taking his clothes off. There weren't very many people on the beach yet, it was the middle of the morning, and I didn't take my eyes off him. He was wearing a short-sleeve shirt with a lightly checkered pattern, hues of white and blue, a pair of tight black jeans that looked rather soft and flexible to the touch. Something told me that this was probably his favorite pair of pants, or more precisely a favorite pair from a rather large collection. First he took the shirt off, unfastening each button one by one, in a descending order. After folding the shirt and placing it next to the book, he unzipped his belt and proceeded to remove the pants. His bathing suit was olive green.

Bowing down in his bathing trunks, he sat on the towel for a while, first lighting a cigarette, a Marlboro Light, with a little matchbook he extracted from one of his pockets. After lighting the cigarette he folded his trousers again, and for an instant he seemed irked at having to repeat the gesture over again. He sat crouching a little facing the lake, smoking and exhaling into the translucent air. I watched the way his lips parted to let the cigarette in, the way his fingers barely seemed to be holding it at all. I was surprised by how tanned his legs were and by the regular pattern his hair seemed to make on his chest, a kind of diamond shaped whorl of brown hair that reminded me of the white marks on a horse's head. There was something a little straight to his movements, a kind of well-bred protestant distance that seemed to sit underneath the seductiveness he projected. He didn't exactly look cold, more like slightly removed, a distance that was as much the product of his race and all the schools and Sunday lunches he attended as the true expression of an individuality. Watching him was like tracking the overlaid movements of class and self, the way they curl and interpenetrate each other into this substance we call a body. He didn't really seem to look around him very much, it was hard to read any kind of curiosity about his surroundings into his eyes, and yet he didn't seem especially meditative either. He was just doing what he was doing, taking his clothes off at the beach, an attractive man of twenty five years or so carrying his beauty like a well-worn coat, something so carefully chosen and considered that he sometimes almost forgets about it.

I wondered about how he looked naked, and I thought how exciting it would be to enter that perfectly arranged space of his, to watch desire shatter his composure. I imagined charting the reflux of control and release, the overlapping waves of distance and closeness, and also the return to the impenetrable wall, the clear veneer, that inevitable part of him. I looked at his hands as he stubbed the cigarette out on the rocks and I knew that this was precisely why I would love him.

Chapter 9

THE RED AND THE BLACK

Am I trapped? Chasing green lights up Tenth Avenue, punching the Guzzi through Chelsea like a fist. I wish I could say a ride in the streets of this city is actually an adventure but I can't. Nonetheless I'm gliding through different cars and worlds. Some are the souped-up ghost buggies from Saturday morning cartoons. Others curb hugging cruisers stuffed with hormone charged teens smoking crystals, with smooth plump thighs that squirm and push against the backrest. These vehicles and more crowd the avenue, and this is the high I get in a city that spells its name M-O-O-D. We are nothing but the illiterate grandchildren of a moldy, Beatnik copulator, self-proclaimed god of the wine-stained mattress of dawn, cheating our way out of the constraints of a structured language that is out of sight, out of time, out for a ride on a Saturday night. Don't know where we're going, but we get there by furiously staying put. Will we ever be able to get there, carve a road to Disobedience? Exit.

A glass eye plunging into the grid, translating concrete and crowds into pure, arbitrary movement, my light found her first, illustrating her bright profile as she crossed the street without looking. And then – Reena Spaulings, out of the blue, a hard fact of the city blocking my way. Minutes ago I was all set to live; now I don't even feel like trying. I feel the happiest of catastrophes is happening to me: Reena Spaulings. All my words transcend into an as yet unseen level of ugliness.

I catch my reflection in the mirrored glass doors. She's sneaking glances at herself as well. Come on, do something besides yawn. But then I look into her eyes and in that second a lever is pushed, the toilet flushes, and I sail down the pipes. There's a conversation under the buildings. Gossip and standing there. Breathing car fumes and the exhaust of passersby. Everybody, pull up a chair and let's watch how these solar assholes get to know each other. Unfathomable ants like you and me, the fascination of boys.

She wanted a change of scenery. I have an extra helmet for these situations. So we went North, Upstate, up the Sawmill, up in smoke, into cold and colder air, cold springs, old trees, and other rustic sensations. I've been there. I'm bored, but I know how to really indulge in soft and fuzzy boredoms.

We stop in a place called Phoenecia. I cut the engine and then it's nothing but darkness and fireflies. She shows me where the tail pipe burned her bare leg, then points up and says, "There's Mars." I'm hypnotized by the dim apparition of her arm in the moonlight and I can't think of one thing to say to Ms. Spaulings.

"Gardsden?"

"Garson," I tell her for the third time.

"Garson, thanks for bringing me here. This is fantastic."

We wander over irregular surfaces, steep angles, hard rocks. Our feet intuiting their way like eyes in the blackness. Into a field. It's as if an envelope is falling over this place, sealing us up inside. There is intention but I try to push it out of my mind. It would be better if this place was a minefield instead of a field, if only to force us to be here and now, force the hand of our presence. Reena takes my hand and squeezes it. I let go, flee her grasp, and then she grabs it again. Now I feel her steps across the tall grass and flowers in the pitch black. I feel my steps as well. I feel loads of unspoken words showering down on me. Shooting star sentences that will never be translated. Swarms of interior monologues, dreads and desires jumping and buzzing around me. This silent chatter makes no sense, these crackling scenes produce no coherent drama.

We are going across this field, trying to get out of it as much as get into it. So then I grab her arm and start to spin her around. Faster and faster, a wide, rotating circle. I shut my eyes and hear breathing, the soft hiss of shuffling feet, and the blood rushing in my ears as I start to get really dizzy, really sick. Reena says nothing, and I imagine her gritting her teeth and getting ready to punch me. We spin right out into the center of the field, smacking a bunch of little trees that break our grip and send us falling. Reena vomits and rolls over in the grass before standing up to take off her clothes. I can only hear these things. I think I am beyond myself, the universe is choking me. I feel a bit absent, but nevertheless, my absence seems to radiate.

Ms. Spaulings consults the mountains before letting me eat her. Please, they seem to tell her as they rise all around. Above us all is twinkling and pointless. Splayed, she lets me inspect her, separate her folds, page one, page two. She's an open book but every turned page presents another cover. I always try to bury my nose in books. Since my nose is too big, it has something to say during oral sex. I breathe out hard through the nostrils, the way dogs do when they sniff people's crotches. I'm congested out here in the downy air. I blow my nose right there, mixing mucous and vaginal fluid. The taste of my own snot, the taste of her juices… I wish she would start peeing right now. My tongue is taking a beating but holding up fine. I guess I'm in shape. It's not like I think of myself as some pussy-eating cop doing exercises whenever I'm off duty. It's just that I like licking ice cream cones. I usually do two a day, a real workout. Furthermore, I like licking cunt. It makes me feel like a pig at the trough. I'm a turtle nibbling away at a head of lettuce. Dealing with multi-layered pastry. Amazing how eating a woman out is an ordeal of tunneling the surface. It takes a superficial man to get to the bottom of it all. No way I can know if she likes it.

On that point, I'm positively blind and deaf, or maybe I don't care, which probably makes me the worst lover she's ever had. Perhaps I cannot even be called that, "lover." And now she's had enough of me. And then I pull myself away. And suddenly she wants a cigarette. She makes objects. She makes action. She offers herself as some kind of trigger. I feel I have been selected for something.

Although Ms. Spaulings presents herself as a soul-baring rebel without a guitar, convincing me of her authenticity is a tough sell for the 24-year-old Canadian-born New Yorker. "Let go!" she screamed. Somehow I didn't feel up to that task, which I understood to be "Prove to me it's worth it." I'd have rather heard another slogan, maybe something like, "Skin yourself alive."

Credibility aside, this "Let go," bolstered by three anthemic, ridiculously catchy singles, established Ms. Spaulings as a scrappy anti-bellybutton priestess, a silk-screened whore of tattered fishnets. It is not clear whether she wants to make us and me believe in her or something or whether this is all a joke. I think the ambivalence is the real mess and in-our-face secret. It is the attraction too.

I followed her into the trees and sat with her in a swarm of mosquitoes. Ms. Spaulings seemed worried that I would dismiss her tough-girl act as posturing. For one thing, she ditched me there and went off in the dark to pee. She was gone for almost an hour. When she came back she continued to refuse my advances. On the surface, she's a hard-rock harangue against a philandering boy ("Did you think that I was gonna give it up to you?" Ms. Spaulings says). I saw you in my nightmares, then I saw you in my dreams. Now I might live a thousand years before I know what that means.

Seeing her for the first time there on the Avenue, I registered an assortment of impressions in a single glance: angular body moving cross-wise, bright red lipstick under street lights, big blue eyes expressing... what? Themselves mostly, but what are eyes but a person's windows? They decorate the building and make it see. I liked her looks and suspected a bright passion parked behind them.

I almost ran her down. What a person wants deep down is to change, but change today is a problem, in this city that neutralizes change by putting it constantly to work and absorbing its effects. Ms. Spaulings seemed not only to allow this possibility but to demand it. It was a toxic meeting.

It's a relief to be out of circulation, out at sea in this dark field. We are the first people, or the people after the people, the Spaulings and the Peterson. You go, you wander, you are lost and you like it. Above, everything goes up and up like an escalator. Below, is the narrative you make up, one page at a time.

I am hard, like a puzzle. My stuff should be harder, but probably it's still up to the task. Reena makes her entire body mouth-like. She doesn't really fuck as much as eat, which I don't have a problem with. To each her own abstraction, I say. So Reena's eating with her whole body and pussy, and I'm timing my thrusts with her big gulps. Lord knows what would happen if I slipped out of rhythm. Something would break for sure. She gets herself off in good time and seems bored while waiting for me to come. I pull out and have her jerk me off. I want to ejaculate on a bunch of dried leaves. I tell her this, and she understands as if I told her we have to pick up a jarful of scattered tacks. This takes almost forever, and I love it. I almost meditate. I close my eyes and listen. Then splat, Reena takes the spermy leaf and plasters it on my forehead. I think I like this girl. She has patience and compassion.

Gazing up into the vertiginous corridors of time and space, looking up from this grassy basement, we were as far from the city as we were close to each other. It's not paradise, it's only two people taking place, side by side, under a tree. Just a place, a taking, a tree, and no more people. I was there. Reena was there. "How romantic," you are thinking. But you're wrong. Romance can never be present, it's always the calculation of previous desires on the bankability of a mentally-designed future. Trying to be present, assuming that presence in the inevitable, irreparable now... how far that is from the dull, absent well of lovers' eyes. Hey! Watch me get rid of all wanting that feeling-at-home-stuff!

I can only be present in short bursts. Whenever I feel something, I turn on the radio. I am intermittent in my desires. I reflect, then get instantly sentimental. My perverse sense of introspection sets in, but instead of getting into myself I'm getting entangled in an idiom: Giving Head. Is it all about that? Then some happy materialism begins to tug at my mental sleeve. Mental materialism is my stud father, whom I loved.

Seattle was a book I used to read over and over and I knew it was all about me, an open heart reading itself in the fog by the sea. New York is an entire library of books about everything and everybody. Reading here is work, and behind every book-filled room is another room of books and the reading never ends. After work I ride to the disco. The disco is expensive. Ride, idiot. Get the hormones going.

I didn't see Reena coming. The city is an open structure that works by calibrating every relationship to its programmed expansion and destruction. We recognize people, we meet, sometimes make love, we read an interview with Rem Koolhaas in a magazine, and in this way we give New York its overall shape. The city needs Reena and folds her into its architectures, making itself rise and shine. Loving or hating her, I am narrating the city, one of its twelve million reader-authors. Narratives parasiting each other, stealing each other's words, names piling up, making noise, filling space. But these are not one story. There is no New York story, only an endless effort to make us forget that narration is war, and that there are at least three New Yorks, sometimes twenty, and countless spin-offs, alles gegen alles. Und alles über alles. Ja, das auch noch!

As we ride back into town, shouting into the wind, Reena describes a new street lighting system for Manhattan. Her idea is to customize the urban ambience by allowing each pedestrian to control the choice of three settings: low, high and off. Three-way switches would be installed on every street lamp in the city. Also, the old bulbs would be replaced with a new type which emitted a sexy red light, and she is sure most people would agree this new glow would be more flattering to more citizens. New Yorkers would loiter longer and talk under the new lights, with the occasional dispute over low, high or off. The police department would do everything they could to kill the scheme, insisting on security. But there would be no going back. Red was the color of New York at night. It looked better, we looked better, and if we didn't like it we could always turn it off.

The next morning opens in the bedroom of an artist's garret. The paint is peeling, but a Marimekko-looking duvet covers the bed. A young man in a trucker's cap (me) sits at the edge of the mattress, fully clothed. Ms. Spaulings is propped against the headboard behind him, half-dressed in a pink tank top and underwear. Except for the pair of skull-and-crossbones knee-highs she keeps smoothing with her chipped black fingernails, the New Yorker's skimpy garb is innocent and girlish. The general haute bohemian gloss is temporarily overwhelming all rationality of the system. As the tender first verse plays out, the young man exits the apartment. Ms. Spaulings takes a drink from a glass of water and hurls it at the wall. This is probably symbolism, but it's also a cue for the drummer to join in for the first chorus. As the band reaches a climax, Ms. Spaulings throws a punch at a mirror – another symbol, more drums, cymbals.

Reflected in the falling shards, we see her expression: anguished but determined to continue to find a way to look right at me and see just about everything but Garson Peterson.

Chapter 10

Two lands, two territories, whose borders overlap. Bedrooms are the site of intimacy. What is more intimate, when shared, than boredom. Boredom is the site of lassitude. Where is there more lassitude than in a bedroom. We at Bernadette Corporation love bedrooms, and we love boredoms. We love couples. We discuss them in our boardroom. Couples are a machine. Most cars are made for couples. The best looking ones are. Even bicycles are, really. So are bodies I guess, but let's not talk about that. Sometimes the less said the better about bodies. Are they metaphors, are they real, are they everything, are they death, is mine yours. Let's be quiet and just shove off with our paddles.

B   B
E   O
D   R
R   E
O   D
O   O
M   M
S   S

Two canoes. Two seats in one canoe.

B is for boredom
E is for enthusiasm
O is for orgasm
D is for drugged
R is for retarded
M is for money
S is for shopping

To Begin:

Experience #1. (Boredom to Boredom).

Boredoms: When you enter into deep conflict between two or more things to do, realize you made a very wrong choice in going to one thing over another. Resign yourself to ennui. No matter your choice, you'll wish you were somewhere else. Which is ennui. Get to it before it gets to you. Boredom like stupidity contains its own treasures. A state of grace providing zero payoff. You'll recognize it. Ignore any path that would seem to give you advantage, in terms of amusement or some kind of good use of the time. Ignore the bong for once. Take your companion outside into the too bright sun. Each of you try to want what the other wants. You'll soon reach an impossible state. Look to the left. Find it tedious. Proceed to the right with the sun assaulting your pates. In consideration for each other, fail to decide what to eat. Immediately on changing the subject of conversation, run out of energy. Understand your partner's agony. Don't give in to understanding. Let the day drag on.

Experience #2. (Enthusiasm to Orgasm).

Now here is the way to go: Isn't it a great day? Take a mild temperature. A late spring, early summer evening. To have a walk. To sit on a roof. Perhaps the Metropolitan museum. To talk a lot. Take in a view. Or sit at the piers. Look at the river. Then get a little tired. Don't talk at all. If you've known each other for a long time you don't need any talk throughout the next steps. Or you pretend you don't know each other, slip into another character. Sometimes it is more fun if you don't know each other intimately yet you might need to map out the body, its character, and how to raise the temperature. Well here you enter. So does your tongue. Kisses are fun. A long kiss can be beautiful. The way a kiss works in a person is somewhat of an index for the rest of the body's sexual manners. A compatible taste and smell of the other body can be detected here. Like a lot of other stuff, a certain seventh sense is required for getting the right dosage here of energy, balance, technique and communication to get the optimum results. But there is always the weather that might ruin it. Sometimes sundowns are just too beautiful and the kiss never happens because everybody is staring into the multicolored most beautiful skies. So in the event that the kiss goes well and you like the lips and the face that goes with it and your limbs seem to move towards each other like classmates and the magnetic field thing starts kicking, motion is required.

Then you walk right into the situation and make out, make love, whatever you call it, make orgasms with or without music. Anywhere. On grass or sheets or floors or planks or sand. A lot seems to happen in bathrooms. But bodies often enjoy better when there is a bit of space around them. Some air to breathe. Orgasm is great release. A great health and beauty treatment, really. Pace and timing should be adjusted to age and enthusiasms of the bodies involved. What should not be underestimated though are the bodies' need, their addiction, building up to spasmic release. The bodies' enthusiasms are ultimately always violent.

Experience #3. (Drugged to Retarded).

You walk hand in hand into the cherry grove. You are feeling good: it is springtime, and the blossoms ransack your amplified senses with their exploding pink, scented, everywhere-ness. The drugs you took are making you tip or slide precariously on your base and you wonder if he or she is feeling it too. The festival of blossoms catches you both, over and over again: let yourself fall into it with every part of you. Your watery eyes are flooding with the pink light and the radical availability of this body that keeps filling your view, showing up in your path or as your path. Go that way. You get tangled up in each other like two branches. Sit down for a bit, on the ground. *Rest your head on his jeans, feel her bony hand in your clean, sunny hair.* You hear other voices floating by. Your voice too, which has gone stumbling ahead while you are still sitting here a little embarrassed, ashamed even, at the way it dodges your brain and at its shrillness. Is it a conversation? Somehow you end up in a sort of eddy together, you and him, and you realize you've been talking about your friend Kate Ballou or the ocean for a long time and that now you are just staring at each other. Or the grass. It stopped somewhere. You both feel this at once and stand up. Have a cigarette, or even better: water. The time might be right to follow the curving path out of the park and hail a cab out on the avenue. Notice how one neighborhood hides another as you roll through the city. Everything is unfolding in the windows. Go home together. Take your shirt off and guide the other's hands over your goose pimply flesh, your nipples, your ass. Make out. Isn't it great that two people can do this? Finish what's left of the drugs. You have to go to the bathroom or you want air. There is a deli just around the corner, usually open late. It is called Mr. Grocery. You can't understand what the man behind the counter is asking you. A bag? Lights? Coins are rolling and he is snatching them up and counting them into shiny, crooked piles and asking you again. How many?

Leave with a bag of stuff. Why is there chocolate milk? Splash it on the sidewalk while tearing it open. Run, on your retard legs. The brown milk is on your shoes and her pants. Fall down and get up again. You can't get up. You twisted your ankle. Your mouth is full of peanuts.

Experience #4. (Retarded to Enthusiasm). Difficulty: moderate, not taxing, but some subtlety.

For Serious Walkers: To get from Retarded to Enthusiasm is to take a step down, Retarded being the highest state and Enthusiasm being the one just below it, between it and Smart. Enthusiasm may be the best place from which to enjoy a view, the view from Retarded being too fluid and that from Smart being too solid. A colloidal state is best, like on those warm cloudy days when everything seems a little soft to the press – sidewalks, door jambs...

How to Get There From Here: look in a mirror. Entertain the wish to know how to pronounce things, in fact a wish to know everything. This will initiate your slide out of Retarded. Stop short of feeling mortification as this will send you into Smart and perhaps through it into Conniving. The stopping in Enthusiasm which is technically a transitional state, fresh as a daisy, requires the slightest little flick of the wrist.

Experience #5. (Orgasm to Drugged).

So it happens. Now there are two bodies in orgasm situation.

They kept doing this orgasm thing every day. It had all the ingredients, the stereotype of a completely self-indulgent affair. Extremely concentrated sex, interrupted by enhanced leisure material like walks, salads, cigarettes, and a little bit of gambling and of course funny talks, lies, jive. It can last up to six weeks. That endorphic high. The orgasmic string. Sex becomes more frequent, more kinky, or sprinkled with violent episodes. One gets drunk through repetition and by the powerhigh that kicks in with the knowledge of knowing every inch of that skin, the muscles, the nerves the twitches, the weaknesses, the zones. One gets to know all possible effects. And learns how to play with them, tweak, combine, shift.

Of course there is no way to stay in that state of existences. Its beauty and intensity lie in its temporality. There is an end to this situation. Some people come down harder than others. Some get really hurt. Some are cautious and check out before it crashes, some like turning it into a downward glide. Try to make pain a beautiful thing too, since you know you cannot avoid the ride. To make this work, one has to be open to it all. Things happen, and some of the things that happen are the wonders of annihilation. Radical disharmonies and the emergence of the Hysterical. As a result there will be also some intense post-orgasmic fuck-you moments. All is worth the effort.

Well there will be a moment in the near future now when one will have to sort of launder the whole image, unless you are proud of the stains, bruises, ambiguities. Still in a kind of daze? Muscles are relaxed now drifting through the simultaneous precision and imprecision of this situation and of orgasms and of music. There we go with 1000 possible unforeseeable sensations still coming up, possibly. The head a speculative bubble, yet permanently scarred. Not yet hysterical enough? It's coming. Now we could make up 100's of uses of orgasms and drugs and of all these 7000 yrs of civilization.

Experience #6. (Orgasm to Orgasm).

After about forty or fifty minutes you pull your brown cock out and come on her soft yellow thighs. Reach down to make sure something really happened and even check your fingertips to make sure, or just to see. You made the Rastafarian come. Lie there and smile together in a cloud of smells. Drink, smoke, admire each other's shoulders, arms, hair, and dried, chewed up lips. Ignore the pain in your pinned down arm. Ignore the time. You say nice things as you admire this and that out loud, or celebrate the act of celebrating the other by repeating yourself or adding things to things, parts to parts, sigh to sigh. Run out of things to say, then sing "Okie From Muskogee" but in the style of Napalm Death. Get water. Get lotion. Get an apple or read to him from the book that's sitting right there: *The Crack-Up* by F. Scott Fitzgerald. Fold your limbs around the other's limbs and bury your faces in each other's sweaty necks. Pretend to sleep. After an hour or two like this, you put on your clothes and go to a show. The band you are watching is called Gang Gang, and everyone is there. Slip out after three or four songs because they are good but you've seen enough. You move slowly through the streets now, with a new little smile your friends will maybe spot and guess at. Hours go by and the smile is still there, but you can't be out here anymore, exposed like this and answering questions. Pass a deli, pass a bar, pass an empty school-yard, pass a pack of drunk, loud, dolled-up weekenders, and keep going past the cop car waiting on the corner. The city is endless and everything is coming at you, moving so fast. Notice his big leather shoes plopping down on the flat, hard ground as you go. Look at the trees, look at the little white dog, look at the McDonald's wrappers blowing in the wind. See yourself reflected in the window of a closed bookstore: it's you, both of you. Soon you are back at your door. Invite him up, she wants to come. Pour a shot of whisky in his ass and suck it out. For the first time in your life, fill a guy's mouth with your pee while he ejaculates on your tits. Drown in those smells again, they are all yours. When you rub her a certain way she starts to moan and squirm on the sheets. You wonder what's really happening, what's going on in his head. When she comes she says it, into you ear: "I'm having an ohgasm…"

Experience #7. (Money to Money).

Money meaning having money. Don't fade out. Start living the way
you thought you might. Start doing things you thought you might.
The way you might. The meat, the night. Spend with all your
might. Money only leads to money, or for a taste for it. Easy money
leads to a taste for easy money. Big money to a taste for big money.
Old money gets in your bones as old money. She comes from old
money. Money operations on the body are irreversible, like time
operations, which is why the two get equated, or at least knitted
together. Irreversible, so enjoy! Go that way. It's an arrow. Don't
deny it. Knit yourselves together in that same seam with your time
and your money. It's a void, nothing but a mirage and total enjoyment. Does money even exist?

Experience #8. (Shopping to Shopping).

You are standing in line with your sisters in the discount store. You
have a handful of nylon-laced g-strings in candy colors and try to
convince the clerk to give you your money back, saying you bought
them just 10 minutes ago and have the timed register slip to prove
it. "So why did you buy them?," the clerk asks, "if you didn't want
them?" You must have just acted on an impulse and you cry for the
manager because there is always a manager behind such impulsive
moments. You can't explain where the impulse came from and it
feels stupid to try. You want to see the manager.

What were the things you always wanted and for what? There
was something but it is not of interest anymore. You feel exception-
ally weird. You want no-things. It is your state of mind now, for
a moment. All exists in undifferentiated potential. The "endless
world" that is of and in the most starkest contrast to the creatures
of the 21st century. You got the sudden desire to make one last pur-
chase, a golden hat. Then no longer feeling a distinction between

the agent and the product of its action you decide you will become gamblers, betting on bets, money for money, shopping for your shopping.

Chapter 11

THE PLAIN LUCY

A fat green pile formed in her hand. She divided the bills between her two pockets. She went out. It's funny that it comes from trees and is still green in the end. They say it grows, but that isn't really the case. It appears, then disappears.

You are free to move around beforehand and afterwards but not while paying. You enter a store and wander around the aisles, choosing what you want, then you stand still and the only things that move are dollars and cents. Try something frozen in this every-day quick-freeze, in this nothing, this embarrassment, this little moment between the happiness of shopping and the happiness of possessing, between enjoying a meal in a restaurant and going back home full. You look like such an asshole, is what Rimbaud said to Verlaine when he saw him walking home with a few bags of groceries for the two of them. That's when Verlaine shot him in the leg. And that's when Rimbaud went to Africa. Cashiers and bank tellers are not sexy, or maybe they are. They are paid to seem unmoved by the money that moves around them in these dilated moments. But they are sexy. I walked by a small bank once on 23rd St. when they were having their Christmas party. The women tellers were dancing in the window, drunk, motioning for me to come inside. They had their half-snazzy bank teller clothes on – blouses, pants; a sharp, half-snazzy dress. Money-workers, sexy.

Was Reena pursuing her desires, or was she inventing them

anew with each ring of the cash register? I don't know. Or was a Reena being somehow "prehended" by her possessions in the same way that the Great Pyramids could be said to have prehended or actively called into being Napoleon's troops many centuries in advance of their actual arrival in Egypt? It was funny. In voodoo rituals the possessed worshippers are like horses ridden by the spirits who jump their available, human bones. But those bones are also what make the rider-gods happen, bring them out of the shadows and into play. Why are we so important to the Gods? Anyway it was obvious to Reena that greater forces were at work here, mingling with her own.

Standing at the top of the flimsy wooden ramp that bent down from the ground floor to the basement in an attempt to be deconstructive, Reena marveled at the aesthetics of a new spending environment. This particular building project had almost everything in common with the faltering brand that had paid for its construction. Its exclusivity lay entirely in the mis-relationship between what it had cost and what it actually was. The price here stood in for any and every other quality. Better than building something that is immediately, visibly luxurious (a hotel with all gold taps for example), building a 40 million dollar plywood shack is at the same time not vulgar and beyond all bounds impressively luxurious (vulgar).

It was a fantastic chain of magic actions by which a girl in an ill-fitting Lagerfeld jacket with a bag full of knives was made to appear, flickering for an instant on the city's screen before flickering out again. Chloe Sevigny picked up some Polos at LaCoste on Madison Avenue. Garson Peterson was waiting outside for Reena Spaulings with two full bags and a slightly stoned smile.

Other Places Nearby (if you're interested): Balenciaga

After an afternoon spent perusing Chelsea's cavernous, chock full of nothing art spaces, stepping into Balenciaga will feel like stepping into a real *something: everything you thought you'd find in the shows – the decadent escape routes, the specialness of a new world in the making, the violence of a bright life forming in the grey heart of the grid, etc. – is actually here. Or is it? A snaking tunnel of an entryway slants down into a vast, sunken area where this season's offerings dangle from simple steel tubes. Anybody who has ever hiked on frozen winter lakes will know the feeling of moving across this raw, unfinished square-footage that serves to off-set the luxurious aura of the garments on sale. Desire and indifference join hands and disappear into the dressing rooms. An oblong island displays creamy leather handbags and other glamorous accessories ranging in price from $300 (a slender beige change holder) to $3000 (a hand-sewn handbag with asymmetrical zippers and a sterling clasp). An igloo-sized grotto with a recessed sitting nook contains nothing but a single pair of sequined sandals, displayed on a halogen-lit pedestal. Other contemporary design features include a video rear-projection glowing faintly on a side wall: the designer's Paris runway show glides by like a dream within its vertical frame. Time takes off on silken wings. On the street again, probably empty-handed, a mounting feeling of futility and dread as you head off to see a few more shows before closing time. Chelsea is like one big parking garage filled with locked-up cars that never move. The recently opened Balenciaga boutique is located on 22nd Street, mid-way between what used to be the American Fine Arts gallery and what used to be the DIA Foundation.*

99¢ Store

Every day something can be picked up. Your house seems the saddest place in the world. So you get out, and go and buy some stuff to decorate, to clean with, to chew on. You lack technique, you lack funds, you lack intelligence, status, you have been up all night, you took too many pills, so you enter one of those stores. It is often crowded. There are a lot like you. There are stale crackers, thongs, plastic sheets, bleach, and lemonade and toothpicks all next to each other. There seems to be no rule for the arrangement of goods. *Every owner or manager of those places seems to do it their own way. Same with the degree of cleanliness or order of the goods. On 23rd between 7th and 8th Avenues you have a display of hierarchies of immigrants going on. The managers are various members of an extended Pakistani family. The boys – and yes they are all males – to watch customers, clean, rearrange goods, are all African Blacks with French Accents. They are vigilant but not obnoxious really. People don't really steal stuff in this 99¢ store. Unless it is some spoiled "rebellious" rich kid doing something for kicks, or a bag lady who is totally out of it, grabbing stuff off the shelves, behaving as if it were her house, a house she hasn't had for over 10 years. You can only pay with cash. Things take a timid step towards transgression when you pick out sponges, underwear, hairbands, a use-once-then-throw-away hammer. Most of the time the place is filled with goods and the aisles are extremely narrow. So there is not really room to hang out. You often bump into somebody, like in a full airbus or a cineplex. Moving fractionally, but you can feel free from all social restrictions in this location. Then buying something there will give you some kind of relief.*

It is the first shop to open in the morning and the last to close. Big red neon signs light up, and you know what's going on: OPEN and again 99¢ and even 69¢, is spelled out in glowing red neon lines. There is a huge wall of toilet paper rolls in the window, and a shop sign crowning it all with one word: Creation. It is a sign that you are without boundaries and alone.

LIQUOR

If you're in the south Williamsburg vicinity, or going by it, and think of getting a bottle, you can arrive at this great seller of liquor, by way of vibrating and jostling over the bridge on the JMZ train or by way of the first exit ramp off the bridge dumping you right at its door or by way of foot.

With cardboard cut-outs of smiling women in tight dresses, a floor filled with bargain booze (including moonshine), a bootleg CD vendor at the entrance, Lotto and Win 5, good-natured workers, energized purchasers with beer bellies and hoarse voices, and the happy counting of meager coins, there's always a festive atmosphere in there. (And conspicuous plastic cups lying about near the workers.) There's always a good mood. As if the ringing up or buying of booze were just like drinking it. Or the interaction with people on their way to a party was like being at one. Expect long happy lines on Friday and Saturday evenings.

Camel's Magic Trampolene

Camel is Parisian by way of Serbia supposedly and runs a falafel stand on 9th St. If you walk through the 4 ft. wide take-out restaurant there's this amazing giant garden in back with a professional trampoline he got from a guy he knew who did gymnastics in the late '80s. He'll let you jump for hours as he brings you diet pepsi with lemon and baklava. As the courtyard is closed off, it's perfect for new lovers who've remembered to bring a sheet and $10 (or else a small potted plant – preferably just about to outgrow its pot). The plants are all kept on a small children's picnic table which is off-yellow.

Juan J.'s experimental music room

Juan is from Mexico City and every morning he lies on his back in bed and flutters his feet to the rhythms of the music playing in his head. It makes very discrete little sounds as his feet brush against the low thread-count sheets – swish swish. He records the sounds with contact mics on TDK 90 cassettes and after performing he makes xerox collaged covers with #s on them and on Fridays from 6–10pm he opens his ground floor east village apartment and he sits there with all his hundreds of tapes on a table and you can buy them for $9 each. You walk in and he says "hi, thanks for coming!" He's always got one tape playing a bit louder than he probably should – little feet brushing against pastel orange sheets. He has

*a Siamese cat named GI Joe who is always smiling. Remember to say hi
to GI Joe – it's very important.*

Chinatown

*The Chinese without ever assimilating Western customs, have become a
very Western custom with their Chinatowns. How conditions of the land,
the disposition of the people, and the experiences they encounter over the
course of their evolution (war or peace, famine, plague, prosperity…)
create such varied human organisms! When there is hardly anything in
common, with such varied ways of being human, the strange production
of cohabitation can seem like inter-galactic encounters.*

*What is between the Financial District and Soho is a veritable zone
of the third world which has been uprooted by some economic wind and
dropped here, where it keeps on happening and adapting in its crazy new
climate. They rightfully sell us faulty electronics, colorful plastic knick-
knacks and fake designer items instead of live pigs and chickens, but how
implacably indifferent they are to us! It's an unbeatable ambiance that
seasons the already tasty flavors of shark fin soup, roasted duck, crab in
black bean sauce, and whatever else is on the menu. The Chinese don't
care: they fart out loud in public. It's not gross or rude or funny.*

Shopping together is like traveling: an elaborate way of making the
couple visible to itself. Dior, Burberry's, Saks and Brooks Brothers
were expertly crafted lenses, and Reena and Garson kept catching
new views of each other in them. This was amusing and stressful.
Trying on a bracelet at Tiffany's, it took Reena several seconds to
recognize her own hairy arm illuminated there under a large mag-
nifying glass. She got a fancy pen instead and enough ink to write
three novels. Garson's corny fantasy of himself was exposed in
Barney's, where he fondled Hermes neckties and tried on a cream-
colored linen suit that was way too Merchant-Ivory, in Reena's
opinion. Look at him hovering around the cuff links and tie clips.

Reena preferred the Garson in the old t-shirt, but agreed that the designer sunglasses and maybe some nice underwear would improve him without erasing him altogether. To accessorize the original boy was enough. If she ever decided she did want to erase this Garson, she figured it would be with something else besides clothes.

The next morning, they awoke entwined together in a ridiculously expensive office chair with many swiveling, articulated, adjustable parts. Behold the retractable cup holders. Ass, spine, the naked couple, embraced in its ever-unfolding, leathery architectures.

"Garson I'm surprised how few show tunes you know. You look like you know show tunes."

"I know. I love show tunes."

"But you don't know very many."

"I know."

"But you're a good singer."

"Singing is a joy."

"Everybody sings."

"I'm surprised how much birds sing."

"Say something you didn't plan on saying."

"…Reisterthal…"

"What was it you were saying about words coming from somewhere?"

"Do words come from somewhere?"

"No, I don't think so."

"A lot of times especially in a show you see people saying words as if the words came from somewhere."

"Why."

"Because we don't believe our own eyes and ears, I guess."

"Should we?"

"Well, say it without it coming from somewhere. There's a barrier, a membrane that separates things from things anyway, isn't there?"

"Garson, I loved what you said about being unbalanced."
"Yeah."
"That was so fun last night."
"I didn't notice it getting light I just noticed that I could see your body instead of just feeling it."
"Yeah. That's something that never would have happened except by the way we did it. The crackers, the Tennyson, the CD."
"We couldn't stop talking in the dark."
"Like frogs...."
"....."

Reena decided to blow the last of her money on something truly excellent. She wanted more than just another thing in her life, she wanted something equal to life. She looked at Garson tossing and turning in his already pee-stained Hugo Boss briefs. She scribbled a note with her new pen and went out. It was a bright, breezy day. The river was shining and bouncing. She emptied her checking account. Down at the marina she put everything down on The Plain Lucy. A couple of hours later, a breathless Garson showed up at the pier in his new sunglasses. They untied the knots. They unmoored. The Plain Lucy's shiny brass horn gleamed in the mid-day sun as they steered her out into the happy current.

"I'll tell you what this boating sure takes it out of you. Can't you look in the hold and see if there's a little something?"
"A little something to eat, you mean?"
"Well, yes. A little something. You know me..."
"There's Vienna Fingers."
"That's what I'm saying."

"You look so cute over there, can you please give me a kiss?"

Oh, there is a lucidity of the stream. Look at that boat on a river. Marine Art is a very specific genre. When fleets of ships were national treasures, and the myth of the fishermen and octopuses still intact, a lot of images with boats and sea emerged. A lot happened in painting. There was a huge demand for the romantic's visions in the motif of the sea and the boat. The most impressive painter of sea and boat was William Turner. Many of his famous paintings are in London's Tate Gallery.

"So who was that guy you were talking to the other night?"

"Oh, I knew you saw that! Well, you know he started tickling me when we stepped outside."

"Where?"

"Right by the car."

"No I mean where on your body."

"It was right in front of Stevie too. I was embarrassed!"

"What did you do?"

"I squealed. What are you supposed to do when someone's tickling you who's never touched you before?"

"I don't know. I don't know what the standard norms are."

"Me neither."

"Fff."

"He kept on doing it in the car too."

"Does he know you're with me?"

"Yeah, but I think he's harmless. I think he just likes me and he doesn't know how to touch women. Or talk to women, once he realizes he's talking to one or whatever."

"What did it feel like?"

"..."

"..."

"I think it was his way of testing the waters. But do you mean beyond all that what did it feel like?"

"Yeah."

"Intrusive but not... unwary?"

"Okay, I know what you're saying."

"It was just his fingers. Had there been whole hands involved it would have been a different story."

"Oh yeah – how so?"

"If we had been alone and he put his whole hands on me?"

Brown wind clouds, a boat, and isn't there also always the idea of the Ark? A deluge too. And beautiful wave movement, and a storm. Ah, the Beauty of Uncertainty. More than 150 years old. This is a most perverse luxury, looking at a boat on water on a painting. Looking becomes the sum of my existence and identity. A painting that contains the experience of the painter watching, observing, painting. Their experience is all over the seascape. Flooded signatures. There it is, a painting flooding with change.

"Jesus."

"I'm sorry."

"What about the sky?"

"I know. I was seeing it."

"Do you think that's a warning?"

"Do you think we could live on this boat?"

"Oh, shit, I don't know. I hadn't thought about it."

Fire at Sea. The skin of the painting crackles with electricity. Perhaps there was human cargo too. It's a scary picture. Its colors, an enormous stimulation.

"AAAAAAAAHHHHHHHGgggggggggg!!!"

One is drawn into the emotion of a drama, directly, no narrative necessary. You really don't know, endless fictions multiply in the yellows and orange. They emerge and insist in sea-passages that might never have been undertaken. Hundreds of them....like *Boats at Sea*, where all becomes pictorial realization of a mental conception. And there is the super minimal watercolor *Ships on Fire* that consists of black, orange and gray blurs, presenting us with the "open secret" of color. The effects of natural stuff, light, water, presented in softly rendered, abstracted shapes. Something that would be potentially deadly in pastel colors. A boat spending time composing the narrative of an impossible death.

"Aye, aye! A strange sight that, Parsee: a hearse and its plumes floating over the ocean, with the waves for pall-bearers!"

It is still and explosive at the same time. A chemical distillation of atmosphere, a shimmering veil that covers everything. All looks extremely artificial. Becoming sensitive to the limitations of the field of vision, you become abruptly conscious of desire, glimpsing, squinting, feeling, ripping things apart with your eyes. You enter new psychosexual constellations, temporarily abolishing rationalism. Letting the body take over now.

"Noooooooo!"

"Jump, my jollies!"

We do not tremble because we feel afraid; we feel afraid because we tremble. Painting is a trigger for a trembling. Observed with a very naked eye. Doing away with contour, doing away even with your formerly cherished verticality. That's the kind of change the world could use more of.

"Kick up de damdest row as ever you can; fill your dam bellies 'till dey bust – and den die."

"Heave-to!"

All this really makes me want to look more at boats. There is a small painting by Helen Torr uptown, a lady painter who was married to the much more famous Arthur Dove. They actually lived on a barge for years and got really sick from humidity and mould. Her painting shows a small boat that carries a few huts. So contained, so sad. She never sailed away. She eventually stopped painting. Also: many, many Ellsworth Kelly shaped canvases make an appearance in Chelsea, and a lot look like sails to me. No boat, just the notion of sailing. Which brings us back to Turner. The notion. What you really see is not the boat but the struggle and some heart burning.

"Ha! Ha!" cried Daggoo with a joyful shout.

There is action. Colliding elements. Somebody not liking it. People who don't care. Sentences spurting out of bodies and boats. One boat approaching the other, like an argument. It's getting closer fast and Reena is standing or dancing at the railing, waving and laughing.

Garson's had it. He feels like the bland mister as a gang of crazy shirtless thugs swarms The Plain Lucy, bangs holes in her and empties their cans all over her deck. Then he doesn't feel anything. He just doesn't want to be involved in this scheme anymore. He is a real expert at turning bland mister. So he does, and dives off the boat!

All this happens in 20 seconds. Garson is gone. He has his ways of making himself disappear. Reena doesn't even notice. The gang keeps attacking the boat. The Plain Lucy is damaged and will sink slowly from now on. Some of the pirates are on board now. They like Reena. They check the boat for any valuables. They take the drugs, the money, Garson's sunglasses, Reena.

The pirates are not really pirates. They are a crew of ghastly hip-looking dudes and gamblers. Part-time dealers of all kinds of illegal matter. The Plain Lucy sinks. Nobody seems to have seen anything, and only when the gang's boat has long disappeared does somebody call the harbor police. And why did the water cops see nothing either? This is a huge unfinished picture. *Fire at Sea*. Going under. Her shiny brass horn gone for ever.

CHAPTER 12

Nobody remembers what happened. What went on in their brains when The Plain Lucy sank, Garson disappeared and Reena became gang-guy-crazy? There's still an elusive spot, a sort of blind one for that moment and what happened afterwards... so all this is a still-desperate attempt to collect data, to reconstruct, grasp a consciousness that ultimately has the status of an object. A reality that would stand for reality. Writing is a serious defense-formation, a mode of repression. There is something thoroughly incommensurable in all this. You can see for yourself.

CHAPTER 12,

In which there is a citywide crisis, Reena disconnects her phone, begins taking medication, and War creeps in. She acts in a movie, experiences loss, changes her name, gains weight, is arrested, spends three weeks in France, meets James Taylor, and experiences a test of will. She gets a new Maris job, loses weight, coerces someone, meets a new gang, is assaulted, watches the sunset, visits Maris's office where she is coerced, and learns a new skill. She has an encounter with male aggression, begins a catalogue of the emotions, experiences loss upon loss, bombs something, more loss, has a death wish, sees her ad for the first time, then goes on a purposeful date, gets sick and injured, loses more, and almost marries a Chinese musician.

$ $ $

This came as a surprise like in a dream: the coordinated rebellion of various groups in various spots in the city. It must have been brewing for some time. Well it had, obviously. Just look at the city, drive through it, and you have to wonder why it hadn't happened before. Well it had happened before, but in some other way not this way. This was something everybody had dreamed about, but wondered if perhaps some kind of a spell had been cast to make it remain a dream. Well, clearly there was, but now the spell was broken. "When you go to sleep your dreams wake up" was one of the slogans seen on the traffic barricades that morning. At certain points along the Brooklyn-Queens border your car might be commandeered or you might be asked to pay a tribute and then be given a receipt. "No Respect" was seen around town a lot. It was like war. Reena disconnected her phone. Following an instinct opposite to that of self-preservation, she began dipping into the medications that had been sent to her by Maris's health service and which, she was told, everyone should take some time between the ages of 20 and 30. It was a plunge into a contaminated pool. She saw a cat successfully cross and re-cross a busy Canal Street. She saw one black and one orange pit bull grazing and shitting exuberantly on a patch of grass. The War, the big war, which was always elsewhere, began to creep in, crying tears of cum out of its eyeballs (as Garson had once described himself). Of course, the troops that were already in the city had to try to deal with the dream situation that was taking place, the No Respect situation, by first "seeming" to deal with it, which was difficult because the No Respect people failed to recognize the army's efforts. It was interesting.

Meanwhile Reena's head shot was making its way around the

city. Maris scheduled her for various casting calls, but Reena only showed up at one or two. One day she appeared in the company of half a dozen of her "friends" – those hooded whoevers who'd been gathering around her like a living crust – on page six of the *Post*, captured from a not very flattering angle as she crammed canapés into her mouth at a movie premiere. There was mention of stolen bottles of champagne and a ruckus on the sidewalk. A black eye, some foul words. The caption under Reena's caviar-smeared face read: "*It* Pig." Maris paled. She begged Reena to clean up her language and see a personal trainer. Reena took offense and told Maris to "cut her some slack, Jack." She dropped out of touch for several days to act in a friend's art video. The thing played on a loop in a "space" in Chinatown five days a week for the following month. As a *Village Voice* critic mused over the slippery meanings and cultural worth of this minor spectacle, Maris spent an insomniac night plagued by low-tech images of Reena "squirting" what looked like a gallon of milky fluid into the air and all over the camera lens. A couple of weeks later, Maris spotted Reena coming out of the Taco Bell on Delancey Street. She had gained 20 pounds and was walking arm in arm with two tough-looking lesbians. They looked happy. Reena had lost her voice in a karaoke bar the night before and could only listen and blink as Maris pleaded with her. One of the girls informed Maris that Reena had changed her name and not to call her that anymore. Her new name was Marcks Engels. Then they piled into a city bus heading East over the bridge. Hot days came, heavy tropical ones that sucked all the air and life out of everything. There was a brown-out in Maris's neighborhood. She lay like a pale corpse in a tub of cold water and updated her Reena file by candle light. In her new press clippings, Reena was getting fatter and fatter. She left a slime trail of gossip and speculation behind her wherever she went. Maris collected and scanned everything. How could she repackage all this as something workable? The sirens outside her window wouldn't quit. In the morning it was birds, but a new, louder kind of bird she'd never heard around here before. Then the phone. It was Reena, calling from the police station. Every shop window on Prince Street had been smashed that night and she was somehow implicated. Maris agreed to put up the bail money on the condition that Reena report to her offices first thing in the morning.

She gets to France. Thank you Maris. Right into Paris. From some previous trips and letter-writings she knows some people there, but nobody with that kind of heavy passion she is currently looking for. All clogged with style. She loves not speaking much French and starts calling everybody "pussy," man and woman alike. Everybody loves that and keeps inviting her to drinks and meals and underground steam rooms. She figures she's got some talent after all, talent for something she doesn't know what it is.

She stays up all night all night, cruising clubs. Pulling out the numbers from one of the ten assistants from the underwear shoot stuck in her passport-protective plastic wrapper, whose hairdresser buddy knows all the hot places. She also got some digits from the gang. It turns out there might be a connection and that somebody wanted to use her as an unknowing spy to steal the campaign. Currently though she is really only looking for some action, like dancing and smoking and practicing foreign flirtation. After a few days she has mapped it all out. For the next weekend there is a trip to a chateau in the southern region, as it turns out one of the fashion scene DJs is heir to this huge lavender export company. There she goes, taking a two-hour lavender bath, followed by a lavender body wrap treatment. She knows that Robert Crumb lives somewhere close by, but decides not to knock at his door. She considers her jugs not big enough. And the DJ wants all her attention now anyway.

There are so many possible pilgrimages in France she could do, but she doesn't really have the energy right now. She wishes she could be like the beautiful freak, gambler, like Isabelle Adjani in the

1981 movie *Das Auge* by Claude Miller. An amazing chain of tricks
and deceits and costumes. A kind of bizarre euro-trash road movie.
Reena feels like a star. Totally. Back to Paris, activating more fantasy and more parties. *Trop tendu!*

A friend keeps talking about shooting this art film in Orléans
and she – taking cues from his existence – takes a train to the town
of the Radical Jeanne and, sucking in the air of history, she runs
into a single older guy who is wandering the town square too and
talks to her in English. Not even asking for directions, he is the
thoroughly disoriented tourist looking for whatever adventure and
a person to eat an omelet with. She doesn't realize it, but she ran
into James Taylor. He even had a guitar. On some benefit-playing
mission. They go to a brasserie and do some chatting, like a lunch
date from the internet or work day happy hour. He pays for her au
lait and a sandwich and before they split he gives her his comeback
CD. She'd never heard of the guy, but takes it anyway. She gets it
to her DJ friend, and commands him to figure out how to extract
a hip sampling from the James Taylor recording. The DJ thinks
Reena is insane but he'd really love to stretch the erratic encounter
he is enjoying a bit more and turns a couple of riffs into this pulsat-
ing beat of events and throws a party. It is the best party Paris has
seen in a while. Even Karl Lagerfeld shows up dancing publicly to
THAT beat. Reena and the DJ know it can't get any better. In the
middle of the glory they celebrate their break up. She is ready. The
gang guy is waiting anyway. Taking her to the river Seine to a small
apartment right on the quai. Two days of uninterrupted medita-
tion. She surrenders unconditionally. From now on she would be
ruled by a belief that it was her true will to serve the secret chiefs
in the evolutionary furthering and liberation of mankind. Maybe.
All things make war all the time. Beauty might emerge from
inevitability. Reena can feel it coming. There it is: Maris calls from
Morocco. She's ready. She is full of conviction, wild with joy. She
sounds like she scored something. Sexually, socially, businesswise,

Reena can't figure it out. Must be a multiple hitting of the mark. It's about producing a movie that deals with drugs positively. But also about a natural beauty product that looks like dirt. The working title for both of her new enterprises at this moment is the same: Foreign Mud. She plans to meet Maris in New York to talk about all the details on Thursday. Her excitement is already oozing out of the receiver surrounding Reena with another layer of glow. Uh, I love Paris. She loves her current state of mind where nothing stable will endure.

Reena's weight comes off as it had come on, in the blink of an eye, like a happy German song heard on the sunny back roads around Munich, with cornfields, bicyclists, oncoming motorcyclists zipping by. When something happens without your perceiving it, it seems to happen so quickly, the way a year passes by. The weight came off like a year zipping by. In her general exuberance Reena found it in her heart to coerce one of Maris's clients into giving her a one-time payment of five hundred dollars for the favor of not destroying the client's relationship with Maris. She also got interested in a new gang, a music gang called the Bass-Viols. Like other music gangs, the Bass-Viols believed in none but imaginary societies. As soon as an imagined society started "clumping," or becoming real somehow they disowned it the way a mother bird kicks out a nestling that was touched by man. They believed that God had been able to excrete us after we had "clumped," and that the only way to storm heaven was to disembody ourselves again. It was coming home from one of their 33-hour meetings or concerts that Reena encountered a middle-aged man who while conversing with her cut her near the armpit with a razor.

Reena watched the sun set as she waited for her tit to stop bleeding. A fox-faced kid she knew from her museum days appeared magically with some iced coffee. Then he was gone. There was music, something Schubert-esque, drifting out of a nearby window, and the sky was going all psychedelic. It was impossible to look at something so beautiful, for ever and ever. Thank god it would only last another minute or so. Among other things, sunsets made her think of funerals and dinosaurs. She went home and cooked herself a perfect omelet with her last eggs, then slept for two days until the birds woke her up soaked in tears. In her dream she had seen Maris crushed under a collapsing building. She threw on something presentable and hurried up to the office. Definitely alive, Maris greeted her with a bony, heart-felt hug and then they got busy giggling their way out of all their previous weeks' misunderstandings. Maris thought Reena looked great. Was it a haircut, the dentist, love? No. Same hair, same yellow teeth, and as for love, Reena said that Maris was the only person she had ever loved. Now it was Maris's turn to cry. The only way Reena could explain the state of grace she'd been experiencing since she last saw Maris was in the words of Simone Weil: the part of her that was being dragged down was making the part of her that was rising go up, like a lever. But why wasn't Reena eating her shrimp cocktail? Maris kept needling her, asking if she was anorexic now or on or off drugs. Seeing no way out of this trap Reena swallowed the fat, cold creatures one after the other as Maris stood behind her and stroked her hair. See? And now she had another assignment for Reena, a TV commercial, but they needed a girl who could walk on her hands and Reena had a hard enough time getting around on her feet. So Maris made a call to one of her contacts at Cirque du Soleil and set up the lessons.

The circus trainer doesn't touch her, but his punches are massive. Almost fainting from anger he stares at her with utter disgust. Ready to slap, punch, kick: tiny clouds of sweaty odor emanate from his body. A funny kind of pollution. Something smelly occurs. Something trying to get through. Still caught up in the rational circuits of exchange and hating it. Perhaps he is still really mad at her because she behaves as if life is nothing but an opiate for life and he feels what kind of mean jilting ally she and her friends are, and how rapid and massive every step is and he feels like punching a hole in the world, the atmosphere, the whole damn thing. Helium high. Ready to partake in a delirium which might vastly enhance his energies. She loves smelling him like this. Although she would not have manipulated him into this mood, she is sometimes a hidden conspirator. Can't help it. So much lies in the body's sensation. To reach the organism directly. To make nerves vibrate with a kiss. The intensity of the sheer proximity of love and hate...

Reena started seeing the emotions come and go as clearly as if they were colors, or fish, and begins to catalogue them: Energized enthusiasms, disruptive dynamics of the sublime, desire desire desire, visualization and concentration, wildness, commitment, lifting and dropping moods, the remains of something before it happens, dissonances, flickering patterns and sonic apparitions, jolts of rhythm. Throughout the night, the wound of incompleteness, sinking, so happy one could kiss the world, psychic revolt, physical revolution, enflamed, cracks in the shield of faith, ecstatic bird, feeling held, incense of genius, sweet, sickly, unnameable, invisible, getting into your nostrils, dappled moments, fragmentary momentary, lulled and soothed, melting and permeating...

Then letting things happen within, where memory and facts mingle. Sentimental cynicisms, mind running in well-oiled grooves, can smell them as I write. Techniques of artifice. Mobile elusive glimmering sense of the world. Hand on velvet, hand on wood, a glimpse of a black pond, bored bird, sweet gloom, everyday life takes the color from the company you are in, possessed, possessing powers of holding people, hands on the jump, a wave of color seems to flow over your whole body, loss of her own story.

So many losses: the boat gone, Garson gone, money gone, James Taylor, the DJ, everybody's gone. Void is. A great exhilaration. She's loving it all. Reena loves losses. Very clearly now, she can see she never liked possessing things anyway, nor felt particularly attached... even before she knew Maris. But since Maris happened and the story and the tornado, she has to acknowledge that she's addicted to loss. What magnificent love there is in all that loss. She remembers now how she lost her favorite big red ball at the beach. She played with it all day long and in the end it sat behind some stack of towels and a small sand dune and she just forgot to take it home. The morning after that she woke up, ran to the beach, but the ocean had taken the red ball away. What freedom. Now the ball was free and she was free of the ball and could go on in whatever mode, depressed, mourning, contemplative or just see it as a chance to find another ball-thing sometime. Prior to our conscious decisions there's already an unconscious decision that triggers the "automatic" neuronal process itself. But consciousness is also bothered by enigmas having no evolutionary adaptive function at all (humor, art, metaphysical questions). The (further and) crucial point is this useless supplement, the compulsive fixation on problems that a priori cannot be solved retroactively enables true explosions of procedures with exuberant survival value.

Time for search, for more loss. But all rules in life have exceptions: there is one thing she doesn't want to lose. That's why she is wearing boots, not sandals. Her passport is in the shaft of her boot. And she doesn't take them off unless she is completely alone in a room. No loss here. Only the idea of it.

Reena was all too happy to plant and detonate a book bomb built by her friend Clovis. She took her rigged copy of James Michener's *Iberia* to the Prada store in Soho as Clovis had directed, but they were shooting an advertisement in there and were closed, so she took it to the Juice Bar next door and let her rip after ordering a wheat grass and ginger. "No deaths," Clovis had insisted and indeed nothing was produced but a big mess. The next day at Kinko's she accidentally cut off the tip of her left index finger while using a paper cutter on the newspaper clippings about the explosion. She couldn't go to a hospital so she threw the fingertip into a wastepaper basket and left. Stanching the flow of blood with a wad of napkins, she wanted to die, on 23rd and 5th Ave., near the park with the statue of Garfield the president. But to want anything, she reasoned, was to be alive, pathetically, and "to want to be alive," even if only in order to die. It was from inside this eddy that she looked up to see, for the first time, on the side of a phone booth, the image of herself in her underwear from the Henry David Thoreau sequence of Maris's ad campaign.

A lot of things were happening now. Sometimes Reena's time felt physically bloated with occurrences. And then nothing would be going on for ten minutes and she felt anxious that maybe the time of things happening was now gone forever. This was bulimic-time, when eight or ten Reena hours became so stuffed with plot and action that the day would suddenly regurgitate its contents and flop at her feet like an empty sack. Sometimes she did things and sometimes things were done to her, and in-between the doing and the being done to Reena was waiting for the "now" to finally announce itself. Her feeling was that the now was not something you could plan or control, it was more like the feeling of a clock exploding. Her body was so bogged down in time. Her body was a clock too. Didn't it feel like it was about to explode, now and then? Then she might feel the now.

After a breakfast date with Garson Peterson (whom she'd lost touch with after The Plain Lucy went down, and who she just knew blamed her for everything – his near drowning, his hospitalization, not visiting him in the hospital, the drugs he started taking when she didn't visit him, and everything he ended up losing, like his job and his sanity, while he was on drugs. Even though their lives had become so incompossible since the boat attack, she wanted to let him know that he was still in her heart), Reena went to meet some of her new friends in their secret hideout and plan some things that nobody else was allowed to know about. Then there was fencing practice uptown, and after that she was supposed to meet the editor of Self magazine who wanted to interview her about the launching of her underwear campaign.

At this moment, Reena was biking through a heavy downpour. She had lost her way somewhere between Bed-Stuy and Crown Heights, way out in the ghetto somewhere, and was obviously going to be late for fencing. Soaked to the bone and out of energy, she found shelter and tried to work her cell phone. It was dead. She should call the guy from *Self*. Running through puddles for a pay phone in the rain, she twisted her ankle and lost all of her change in a really deep puddle. Where was her wallet, where was her bike, where was the phone she was just running for? She felt it, that she, whether she liked it or not, was an entity that questions its own being, she also felt the elusive factor X that accounts for the difference between states. The rain seemed to be washing everything away. Suddenly she felt feverish. Her ankle might be broken, which was a shame because tonight she might have to do some running. She flagged down a car and begged the driver, an elegant Chinese man, to take her to the city. Delirious Chinese string music was playing on the stereo. Singing along intricately, the man offered Reena Newport Light after Newport Light as he chauffeured her uptown. The cigarettes, he confessed, had been dipped in opium. When she tried to pay him, he didn't want her money. He wanted her to be his wife, and he smiled and nodded his head, watching Reena deliberate over his unexpected proposal. He watched the idea of the two of them together, maybe naked, maybe forever, turning over in her face which was getting pinker and pinker. Reena was about to say yes, but then said no and got out of the car. Changing her mind again, she turned back to the car but it was already disappearing into the rain. She hobbled into the Loews Cineplex where Maris was waiting for her.

Chapter 13

THE BODY LEAVES THE CHAIR

Frayed ass-less leather chaps sliding off sweaty horse flanks. Reena gapes, checks her watch, then gapes again. Slit throat sun igniting brambles, endless bloody scrub. Kicked up dust and dark, swollen synthesizer, my Lord. Maris feels unhinged, as open and dust-blown as all that lies before her.

"I ain't been to town for quite an age. Tho' I reckon this town don't look like much, plenty a buildens, plenty a folk. No place to git any provisions or vittles, no one friendly enough to invite y'in for some grub an they send the sheriff out after ye 'f they see y' fixin to make a campfire. Walk out five miles on foot for some banker boys whisky an no kind word. Plenty a green grass an no horses to munch it."

A series of flat graves, flush with the ground, or sunk below the ground, with grass creeping around and nearly swallowing the stones, the stones blackened and begrimed with scale.

"Yeah, it's lonely to be a cowhand, you know? Huh? I know they always say that but unless you're REALLY busy, no matter where you are, you can't help but end up looken out into the distance far, far ahead of you and all around you."

The cowboy stiff-arms the cemetery gate with the load of another "dead" cowboy under his arm... A breeze is leveled straight across the graves, as if out of a blowdryer. Dust deposited into the engraved names of Archibold Harrington, Henry Orrin Ashlock,

Clement V. Tubbs, Violet "Little Mama" Haley, Doris Post...

"Just a' looken an' LOOKen."

He darts across the cemetery lawn, dodging left and right, running a pattern that even casual fans of football might recognize as the "'47 Notre Dame Y-fork." Penetrating the deepest, darkest cluster of tombs, he lays the lifeless "corpse" down on a slab, and does an extravagant end-zone victory dance – squatting and waddling, arms flapping, thigh-slapping, just short of laying an egg and crowing. Meanwhile the dead cowboy begins to stir and then sits up, maliciously blank-eyed. His movements speak of zombie slowness and zombie singlemindedness.

"I reckon I need m' space, but once you start in to all that looken... I sometimes can git lonely jess looken downward toward the grass or at some lowly insects on the earth. Sometimes I'm jess desperate an I cry out, 'I'll take anyone for a friend! Just come along! Just appear to me!' 'Hurry!'"

The first cowboy, a fine and alive athletic specimen, notices the transformation of his sidekick and punches him back down. The undead one hits the slab with a skull-cracking thump, once again inanimate. Satisfied that that is the end of that, the cowboy turns away, forgetting his dance, looking in the distance for something like a lost thread.

So now for the fourth time...

"Dang, m' leg!"

Blood and chewing tobacco runs down tattered and frayed ass-less leather chaps as the big burly, decaying mustachioed cow wrangler wearing a train driver's cap frenetically shakes his head from side to side, teeth clamped around an equally bearish, equally mustachioed horse-riding cowboy's buff, hairy calf. The frenzied semi-Siamese duo riding into the sunset (of the dead) as the biter's dragging, wriggling body whoops up a trail of dust...

"I don't want any friends. They won't know how to treat me. How to touch me. And if I have a friend, I'll need to be touched. And in the right way! Don't just jab at me, friend, GRIP me. Keep it on there nice and firm. Careful not to tickle m' hide by stroken too lightly, and don't vex m' flesh muscle-meat by a lot of un-introducted jabben/grabben."

The previously warm-blooded, heart-throbbing cowboy is now plunged into a trance while his body outwardly transforms. His skin flakes off and discolors into zombie skin. His clothes fray into zombie rags. His teeth protrude into flesh-rending Zombie teeth.

"And don't call me on the phone. If you want to see me, come on over – just give me a holler when you see me. Once you find me, don't ask me a lot of questions. Don't PROBE me. But don't be uninterested in what I'm tellen you either. And it's okay to just sit without talken."

He unhooks a mysteriously-glittering amulet from around that same cowboy's freshly-zombified, stiff, rotten green neck. A ghoulish grin cracks his leather face as he places the amulet around his own neck.

"I've had a friend come along, try to find SOLUTIONS to m' problems instead of just listenen to me complain. They'd end up lecturen me, tryen to boss me or tell me what I SHOULD do. I SHOULD look at it different, I SHOULD take some sort of action agin m' problems, I SHOULD go to a church or stop thinken about m'self s' much, to start to thinken of others. Don' tell me what to do, friend."

He leaps to the ground, executing a sharp triple flip and roll at the same time. With what can only be an enchanted agility imparted by the amulet, he then alternates tiptoes and leaps to shoot himself across rows of headstones before grabbing a stocky tree branch and catapulting himself over the cemetery wall.

A third man now enters the cemetery, unaware of the things taking place. He walks decisively as if on some definite sort of business. And what business it is, as he rounds the corner of a modest mausoleum! Perching on the surface of a slab decorated with a statue of a weeping angel, he drops his pants and crouches in the position as if to lay a shit right at the angel's feet and smother up the name of the occupant of this soon-to-be defiled tomb. But there is a fatal chink in this man's nonchalant boldness and defiance: he hazards a cursory glance around to make sure there are no witnesses, yet only a scant few yards away stands the still-immobile, now fully-zombie-looking, cowboy, terrible and tall, ready to unleash flesh-eating death in any minute. The grave desecrator hoists up his trousers and speeds off in terrified haste.

Your teeth open gulfs between stars, inside God, my Lord. There is only twilight now that God has been passed over by us, a twilight that is the true dawn of the dead, for there is no longer a place for the dead when they die... We mourn, as always, but no longer for the dead; instead, only for ourselves, those who are left behind.

Maris reminded herself, while watching this incredible movie, one of these new westerns from Ghana, that she shouldn't be envious of the African movie industries or the Hindi movies, the Cambodian movies, all of which were so fresh and large, so alive, so able to use the American movies if they wanted to, the whole American body, but without really needing to, so able to occupy, to colonize the spacious American "mind," for their own convenience! But hadn't we produced *Grease*? That gorgeous, enviable, white, pink, and black ball of energy? There's nothing more Baliwood than *Grease*!

Cut to:

A medical chart, the graphic results of an exam. Out the window, the top of a palm tree. Breeze. You can't tell if it's gray or sunny outside; the glass has a kind of haze, but it's not tinted. Chatter in the hallway about wildflowers, the Texas panhandle.

The top of her head is not much higher than the doorknob on the door that this child-sized woman pushes open so as to enter an operating room solely occupied by a comparatively large woman who appears to be playing with an assortment of plastic bladders lying on a trolley beside the operating table, upon which the short woman leaps, so that standing there on the table her eyes are now level with the eyes of the large woman whose feet are planted on the floor. With a nurse's authority and indifference, the large woman lifts up the hospital gown the short lady is wearing, now practically not wearing, as the nurse's hands feel-up or examine the short woman's little breastlets as words are being exchanged between the two.

"Okay, just lie on back and I'll start the measurements. That's good. When was the last time you had this checked?"

"About two years ago."

"You should really have this checked more often than that."

"Like how often?"

"Every six months."

"Two years isn't that much longer than six months."

"Okay."

"Not when you've got an HMO breathing down your neck."

"Yeah, I hear you."

"So how is it?"

"This job?"

"No."

"Oh. Well, we'll have to wait for the lab results."

"Come on. Don't give me that crap. You see this all the time, you're so familiar with all the different situations."

"Whatever."

"You can tell me exactly what's going on just by looking at it. I know how you people are. You can but you won't. You don't want to have to deliver the bad news. So you just do your poking around and jabbing this into that and then you take your gloves off and go on your lunch break."

"Thanks, I will."

"Fucking Jew!"

"I'm not Jewish. Put that down."

"Oh, you're not? What about this!"

And quicker than the end of a sentence a large floppy silicone breast bag is grabbed by the short woman and swung at the large woman's face, slapping her across the chin. The large woman raises her fist with a certain menace of smashing the small woman's face but is stopped by a shiny sterilized scalpel from the same breast trolley and brandished by the furious, short patient.

"I already said put it down. I can call security."

"Go ahead, bitch. You Jew bitch."

"Okay STOP!"

"No way, bitch!"

"Hey–"

"No way in HELL!"

"Please. Please put it down."

"Oh, now it's 'Please. Please put it down.' Not so tough now. Not so in control now, huh?"

"You're the one who is going to lose control if you're not careful."

"No fucking way. Now it's party time!"

"It's not too late to turn back, but almost. I'll just need some help in here–"

"No way in HELL bitch."

"Room 514. NORTH! North."

"You and me, we're goin to the end of the line!"

"Jesus. Oh, my God. Can't anyone… Call security! Call security for God's sake! Call sec-uuurity! Ha! That's it, get the lead out!"

The large nurse flees out of the operating room, past waiting and supply rooms, dodging orderly-shuttled gurneys, past shut doors with machinery humming inside. Down the hospital's corridors the large woman huffs and puffs, her now very noticeable large breasts bouncing up and down from mid-sternum to just above the clavicle, breathing even more gaspingly and over-worked as she pushes herself to put some distance ahead of the dogged short woman running in a straight iron-willed line of nerves, arm raised high with scalpel poised to strike.

The assailant's stocky legs move so fast as to create a futurist dachshund blur while the rest of her body is immobile, a fordist torso with one bright, shiny foo kyuu brand meatcleaver scalpel being pushed along from below. The big hulky figure in front is in a running panic flailing, falling, leaping forward.

The corridor is underground and endless, connecting the old wing of the hospital and the new wing. Light pulsates and must be coming from somewhere, but where? The linoleum is poorly laid or just old, curling at the wall edges, and freaked with teal. At long intervals there are prints on the wall, with splatter-pattern images, also mostly in teal, but somehow at odds with the linoleum.

A basketball player or a very tall man wearing a Dallas Mavericks basketball jersey is doing some wobbly leaning against the wall.

Suddenly the conveyorbelt killer torso stops dead in its tracks, cleaver dropping to the ground, face lightens up and she walks back carefully retracing her steps.

Meanwhile, a basketball player or a very tall man wearing a Dallas Mavericks basketball jersey is doing some wobbly leaning against the wall as the large nurse flees through and past the corridor, making him wobble even more and raise his hands up in defense against this unwanted hallucination which in no time decides to interrogate him in the form of the short woman who brings herself to a complete stop, staring at him in a disbelief turning into recognition as she throws her weapon down and approaches the staggeringly incapacitated basketball player who is clutching and exploring the surface of the wall instead of acknowledging this smiling woman-child who is addressing him by name and asking how he is doing, to which he responds by trying to smother the front of his face into his armpit heedless of the growing insistent entreaties and questions coming from the innocent-faced short woman whom he waves off with an angry spin before stumbling and weaving away, far away from here.

"I'M RRREALLY…OUT."

"Marcus, it's me. Let's go back. Okay? Right now…"

"DO YOU KNOW WHAT TIME IT IS? I CAN'T FIGURE IT OUT. I THOUGHT IT WAS LATER? HUH? WHAT?"

"Let's go back. Do you understand?… Okay?"

"MY KIDS… I DON'T EVEN KNOW IF I EVEN HAVE KIDS LIKE I THOUGHT I DID…."

Quite disappointed, the short woman looks to pick up where she left off, bending down to recover the dropped scalpel and walking to a set of automatic doors that open out to the parking lot where she finds the sweating large nurse on all fours, catching her breath and calming down. Letting loose a sharp yell, the short woman barrels down on the large woman, who once again is forced to propel the unwieldy weight of her body across unbearable distances.

"This isn't fair. This isn't FUCKING fair…"

Nearly gashing her plump thigh on a pebbled garbage receptacle, which flares outward at the top, inert, immovable, impossible to move even if somebody had the good sense to do so.

"Howard!"

"HOWARD!"

The breeze has no sound, as if seen through glass, with only the occasional rattling from an air conditioning unit. On street level you can see strands of hair whipped into girls' mouths and their fingers coming to pull it away and imagine the taste of the hair.

Reena stared into the screen, but the movie kept falling from her eyes. The sound was quite well installed and kept her senses almost too occupied. She sat there. The cloth of the seat in front of her was worn. She looked at Maris's skirt next to her. She had the shiny kind. Not worn at all, shiny-new. The action on the screen was getting wilder. Not really wild. The usual wild in an action film, like the chase and the shooting sequence. And some kind of cathartic collapse coming up. Of the kind you never know why, for what purpose. Just happens...

A large midtown hotel. Casually ambling past the over-stuffed efficiency and boredom of the lobby, the zombie cowboy wearing stolen cowboy hat and stolen amulet grins politely at everyone he sees. Even so, the bellboys, business travelers, wealthy newlyweds, waiters, dressed-to-the-nines clowns from a clown convention, newspaper vendors, and bartenders don't seem to notice him at all. Looking down, we see that every guest in the lobby traipses through sand, as it covers the entire immense lobby floor. Periodically, workers rake the sand evenly over bare spots around an artificial beach where waves wash against a sand bank. The motor propelling these waves is loud, hurtling the waves from black caves on either side of the lobby. No one seems to even react when the lights of the hotel flicker on and off in time with the far-off rumble of cannons and bombs that jangles the nearby crystal chandeliers. No one except for some journalists who gulp down the last of their gin fizzes, heft their video cameras over their shoulders and plunge out into the information-heavy streets. Birds hover high inside the lobby. Pigeons, and something bright. Parakeets. In one corner is a deepwater pool, cordoned from the rest, a pool for high divers. Every once in a while one of these sour-faced denizens emerges from a cave and scrambles up a guano-encrusted volcano for his next dive. They climb through the warm steam drifting across the air, which is steam generated by an artificial cloud maker.

By now having ambled over to an isolated grove of low tables and plush armchairs, the cowboy zombie spots something interesting: a fresh newspaper bearing the front-page headline ALL HELL BREAKS LOOSE, and sitting on top of it: clear but smoky glass, the bottle is simple with the exception of its stopper, a late 1800s carved ivory figure of a wood chopper taking a short break with a bottle while sitting on top op a pile of branches he just cut. The figure is monochromely ivory apart from light pink dots depicting a rash along his neck, back, knees and upper thighs. Inside the bottle, creepily mirroring the ivory figure is a small, trapped, actual man, an incarnation of the old superman cartoon character (who in turn was an incarnation of an old mystico-mythological character) Homunculus. Beside himself in disbelief, the zombie removes his cowboy hat and wipes his brow, accidentally scraping loose a chunk of rotting forehead that falls to the floor. He laughs out loud as he hoists himself up into the armchair nearest the bottle and newspaper, and then, suppressing his laughter into some gleeful chortles, he cheats his found treasure all towards himself, like the rightful owner he now is.

He, he, he. Hey man…. Got…to…touch…..power…… Yeah, this is music, this here, behind your eyes: dah da dah, dee dee, and away we go! You the composer who listens to the prodigious concerts of the soul, without ever laying a single note on paper, hearing only…

A blast. Shouts. The air filled with clouds. A horrible smell filled the theater.

…only the sweat gather behind the neck and in crotch, plus limp dangling cock, that smell of frying mushroom…

"Well, if things are going to be like this I don't think anyone should mind if we smoke too," said Maris as she fished a bent Parliament from her handbag. "The film's not *that* bad… It's not exactly *Citizen Kane*, but…"

Maris was having trouble breathing and seeing. The emergency lights were on but the lit up smoke was even worse than darkness. She stayed in her seat and added her smoke to the smoke, waiting for the air to clear.

But then something fizzled thru the air, the screening still continued but there were actual bodies jumping up in the seats, and the bodies started screaming too... Bits and pieces started falling down from the ceiling. The air was getting pretty bad. There must have been a foot-thick layer of asbestos-rich matter in the wall padding. People, almost blinded by the fine ugly matter, were jumping and climbing over the seats. Apparently everybody fell into purgatory in an instant and couldn't handle it. Of course, if we could have handled it, either it wouldn't have been purgatory or we wouldn't have been in it. There's no handling the purgatory that you're in, or the movie that you're in.

Maris wasn't in the mood to run. She hated running. She was wearing heels. Everybody was running. There was a blast of smell. Smells like metal and sweat, adrenalin pouring into the room. Reena also smells that particular patchouli-scented body spray that Maris is using. Some kind of neo neo hippie thing but made for the career woman. At least that's how it had been advertised. Some new product. How Maris always goes for new product all the time. Reena cannot believe herself that she is thinking of Maris body stuff while all this is going on. But then Maris is the person closest to her in a moment that could be the last moment of their lives. So why not. And besides her senses are telling Reena what to do. More than anything else. She experiences the highest sensitivity possible. Activated by whoever whatever. Was it a gang? Was it the movie? She recognized it so much that she couldn't identify it.

New worlds are coming out of you now, messy ones with emotions attached, and you would blast anyone who tried to block their coming. It is exactly like war when this happens. Right now your world happens in a ball of lit-up smoke. You are so beautiful, moving in your cloud. We just can't understand you.

Somebody was tagging the screen with black spray paint. Her arm moved in rapid swoops across the empty rectangle. She was riding on another's shoulders, squirting out confusing words that looked like strings of black flowers. Then the lights switched off again.

"Reena!" Maris is full of love for her and the whole situation. She could kill her if she wanted to. But that idea did not fill her with so much joy today.... She was having an allergic reaction to something... her lungs, her skin. She lost one of her heels in the commotion. She lost control of her bladder. Somebody bumped her from behind and all the stuff in her handbag was on the floor getting trampled and kicked around. She went into a crouch and covered her mouth with a Kleenex. She closed her eyes and calmed herself by breathing in, breathing out. She started to piss. And laugh. The river of piss snaked between the seats and made a little lake under the screen. Security guards dragged her out into the lobby. Pissing... one heel dragging...

"Let go, monkey..." They let go.

All the cops were looking at her. She smoothed her skirt. She got up and got out. Then Reena was there too. They got out, it was fine.

Chapter 14

DIE GEHEIMRATSNATUR

As for the order under which we lived, everyone knew what it was: Empire was staring you in the face. That a dying social system had no other justification for its arbitrary nature but its absurd determination – its senile determination – to simply *last*. That the world police had been given a free hand to take care of anyone who didn't walk straight. That civilization, wounded in its heart, no longer encountered anything in this endless war but its own limits. That this headlong race, already a hundred years old, had produced nothing but a series of more and more frequent disasters. That the human masses had grown used to this order of things, with lies, cynicism, exhaustion or drugs, no one could pretend to ignore it.

Rattled and begrimed after the commotion at Loews, Maris went home and took a long, solitary bath with candles, then dialed her favorite male escort service and ordered a muscular Tom Cruise. Restless Reena went to Waste, which had been commandeered by a new crop of club kids that was waging a campaign against DJs, videos, jeans and couples, among other things. The new doorman, Peter Teets, stood at the entrance in a shoplifted three-piece suit, enforcing the new what's hot, what's not plan. Reena made her way down to the wildest room, and saw that a new idea of wild was in effect. It was not the normal orgy. The place reeked of chemicals, sulfur, and long work tables had been set up where the dance floor used to be. Where was everybody? The skate ramp had been burned to the ground, leaving a new pile of ashes, which Reena stepped through on her way to the bathroom. Checking herself in the mirror, she heard a violent argument between three people in one of the stalls, followed by an eruption of laughter. Exiting the bathroom, she noticed a freshly dug tunnel, leading who knows where, guarded by a Paris Hilton look-alike with a radio headset. Reena made her way to the "back room" where she stumbled upon a silver-haired gentleman with a necktie and sadistic-looking black boots, sitting all by himself in the dark. He was wearing dark sunglasses. He was Karl Lagerfeld, the famous German fashion designer.

Reena Spaulings: Can I sit with you? I can't seem to find any friends in this place.
Karl Lagerfeld: Please.
RS: You look exactly like Karl Lagerfeld… but *exactly*.
KL: Thank you.
RS: You are Karl Lagerfeld…?
KL: I am Karl Lagerfeld.
RS: Really? You're shitting me, right?
KL: Doubts are like a cold. You can get rid of them.
RS: That's beautiful. What else?
KL: Self-indulgence is suicide.
RS: You look great, by the way.
KL: I'm never totally content with what I do…that's my beauty secret and also the key to my longevity.
RS: So how come you're hanging out at Waste?
KL: I do everything by following my instincts. I have no preconceived ideas or principles. I just wandered in, really. Everything tonight has grown together, like trees growing. It's hard to explain and it is not necessary for me to analyze myself.
RS: Where is everybody?

KL: I don't really care. Whatever I do, wherever I am, I have this self-confidence that's built on a deep, general mistrust. I have no mercy with myself and I am "distant" with myself, even when everything seems a hundred percent personal.

RS: What were you like when you were my age? Did you hang out?

KL: Of course.

RS: So what kind of a kid were you?

KL: I had a vision. A childishly deep conviction. I was different from all the other people surrounding me and I liked that. I felt something Special was waiting for me. Whatever it was and however it would occur, I knew it would happen. I remember it very clearly: I was living in exile from life. Bizarre it was, Ms. Spaulings. I still see the space in front of me, the room where I was sitting when this thought occurred to me for the first time. It was ca. 1945 on the Bissenmoor Estate (that particular guesthouse has since been torn down). I was sitting in the expansive bay of the "ladies chamber," at my mother's desk, which was not my place really, but I loved the "adult world" so much. That's when the idea emerged, the idea of an unknown, exciting, legendary, promising place just for me. Perhaps I had been reading too many fairy tales, who knows?

RS: Yeah. Well I'm still surprised to see you here. It's not as glamorous as it used to be…

KL: Where should I be? If I don't get out sometimes, I'm just hobbling around in my own misery, in my own style. For me there's a logic in stepping forward into new situations. It also happens that I leave things and people behind, when they can't keep up with the pace. I have no mercy. When I was a child my mother told me, "compassion is a weakness." I've found this applicable to myself and to the world. That might sound mean, but at least it's honest. I like to keep my process constantly open to change, otherwise I'm dead. In certain moments, only a radical change can save you from becoming "vintage," a "period piece." I like to think of myself as a kind of Orlando, as in Virginia Woolf.

RS: Do you like art?

KL: I love Picabia's work from 1915–1920. I hate his late, bad painting. But as a guy he must have been quite ravishing in his times. I knew Andy Warhol quite well. There are people who keep comparing me today with him then, ridiculously. My world was an unspoiled almost idyllic and affluent world. He built his world out of a very poor and somewhat ruined world, then formed a whole new generation – like an activist, almost – and then moved up in society, became *mondaine*, a world that at that time wasn't as vulgar as today, mind you. This was before *People*. The world today is so boring. Re-read his texts in *Interview* from 1969–1979. Nobody today would dare writing or talking like this.

RS: And didn't you know Coco Chanel?

KL: In the beginning I knew nothing about Coco Chanel. Chanel was not *en vogue* at all then. Also, time adds another dimension to the "personnage" factor. What we imagine and what I liked in regards to Coco Chanel have nothing to do with reality. For those who come after, the idea of things is often much more important than what really was. That goes for people, places, times.

RS: Why do they call you "Kaiser?"

KL: John Fairchild called me Kaiser before anybody else. Was it a compliment? I'm not sure. Wilhelm II was a very bad Kaiser! He was known for his extreme vanity; a lonely decadent parading around in fantastic uniforms.

RS: How much space do you allow for chance when designing a new collection? Do you plan things out or do you allow for "lost moments?" Do your creative procedures vary? Is it working itself that inspires work?

KL: It's a question of balance. There are no rules, really. "Inner voices" can be helpful at times, otherwise there would only be "marketing." My motto is: Doing for Doing Itself. I can forget Goal and Purpose for a time. That's my idea of artistic freedom, if

I were to consider myself an artist.

RS: Do you have to force yourself to get to work sometimes or is it always a kind of pleasure?

KL: Oh, it would not be possible otherwise. People today seem to have a negative vision of the word "work." Of course I have the privileged position of a person whose work consists of what interests me the most. I find myself a lazy character, and I waste a lot of time reading and daydreaming. But then, perhaps that's necessary for creativity...

RS: Are you a dandy?

KL: The term "dandy" is utterly alien to me, in regards to my person. The Poor Word! The Poor Fellow! They have been made responsible for a lot of things....

RS: Is it hard competing with youth?

KL: Youth is not necessarily the competition. Too many "young designers" have proven that they were only young and not much else. They come and go all the time. When I was young, youth was not in demand. You had to prove that you were good and not only young. But competition is stimulating and essential – even now that the game is so heavily manipulated by the extreme capitalist structure of the the fashion-world. And of course I do profit from that. So does Chanel, LVMH, even H&M.

RS: What made you say yes to the H&M job? Was one of the incentives perhaps the lightness, the possibility to play with your persona, position, kaiser-ness, more than you could in other collections? I noticed your signature all over the place, and the "Liquid Karl" perfume, even a Karl-like-a-rockstar T-shirt for $15.

KL: It's simple: H&M is a fashion phenomenon of our time, and somebody like me cannot ignore this. Their success was not foreseeable and did change something in the world of fahion as well as in the reception of fashion, as well as for the people who work in it, including myself. Suddenly we find ourselves in the 21st century and the ways that fashion is spreading are different and very fast.

The only thing to avoid is the middle. The Mediocre. I find myself very happy now with this success and I would have loved it if even more people profited from it.

RS: I find it fascinating how you design as if there were nothing to lose and everything to win. Your strategy seems based on the grandeur of the casual throw.

KL: 100 percent YES, and I take this as a compliment. Even when things are of course naturally complex, it is part of my profession as well as my character to produce a certain sovereign impression of "lightness."

RS: What's up with the fan, the hairstyle, the dark glasses, the tight neckpiece? Are you trying to set an example?

KL: Is it perhaps an invented figure, my version of the Commendatore in *Don Giovanni*? Perhaps. People think I've always been like this – but that is not correct. Only your last impression is relevant... until the next "expression" kicks in. It's not easy....

RS: You put out such catchy slogans, lines that stick. Like in a good drama!

KL: Life as I live it is like a stage. But often you are alone, waiting around for lengthy periods of time in your dressing room or in the wings, getting ready to act and to be spontaneous again.

RS: Do you ever go to art galleries?

KL: Today catalogues and reproductions are of such great quality that they are sufficient. You really don't need to see the original. All artists, the old ones, the new ones, avant-garde-art, all that is primordial for me. I want to and must KNOW them all. I keep seeing and learning. It's my insatiable appetite.

RS: Thanks for talking to me, Mr. Lagerfeld. You're a great conversationalist.

KL: I learned that from my mother, then it was refined through many many steps. I talk a lot, so I don't need to say much, because I am thinking. As Voltaire put it: "That which needs an explanation is not worth an explanation!"

RS: Do you differentiate between those people who are bored and those who are not bored?

Is there a dream of ongoing creativity directly connected to, inclusive of all of your activities – like dancing, writing, bleeding, social obligations? Are there priorities? If there is no designated "leisure" time, but everything is work, even non-work becomes work. Are you a workaholic?

KL: Well that is certainly my tendency. But that's how it is. One has to be engaged 100% in whatever it is and however complex it is. That's my conviction and my nature. Perhaps it is a "talent" or something I inherited... I don't really know where it comes from. But it is in me, it's natural, effortless almost. These are advantages that not many of my colleagues have. Maybe it is also a question of background and education.

RS: What else?

KL: Sense of life is Life itself! 100%!

RS: What do you think about Europe?

KL: "L'Europe des Lumières" is my ideal – not this European Union, this materialism with no Spirit or *Charme*.

RS: Where does your love for uniforms come from?

KL: Uniforms need to fit well. When I talk about uniforms I'm thinking about the ones in old photos or paintings, not real or contemporary uniforms. There was Glamour and there was Color. Today it seems uniforms are all dark and with no *éclat*. I fight That! I hate the military, but I love the uniforms. Deep down I'm a *Geheimratsnatur*.

RS: A what?

KL: A certain kind of authority that existed in the pre-democratic Austrian/German bureaucracies: tough, judgmental, stylish....

RS: Yeah? Were you raised that way?

KL: My mother had two Ideal Men, whom she admired strongly and she thought of as models for myself: Walter Rathenau and Count Kessler. That is VERY "Wilhlemstrasse." My mother was the daughter of high ranking Prussian Bureaucrats. I would have gone to Berlin, if there had not been the War and the Nazis. "Born way too late," she always said... that...

RS: Are all of your activities part of a continual process of self-realisation?

KL: Very Yes! But I owe a lot to my parents. And then there is my very balanced, almost puritanical, healthy nature, which doesn't really sit on the surface, is less visible...

RS: Do you like drawing things and if so why is that?

KL: Drawing is the starting point. It starts there and it often also ends there. I can draw really well, and it helps me enormously to express quickly and with clarity what I want. It is a great advantage!

RS: What about painting?

KL: Yes, very interested, but time and talent are lacking. My influences: Jawlensky, Matisse, Kandinsky, Feininger, all Expressionists, Manet und Goya, Poisson, Philippe de Champaigne and the religious painting of the 17th century. I love the 18th century, but that's more in relation to fashion.

RS: Do you prefer working solo or in a team?

KL: Both. First I work alone and prepare, then I expand and work everything out with a team.

But the structure of the company itself bores me, even my own companies, with the exception of KL, the shop and the publishing house.

RS: You have a romantic idea of creativity...

KL: I think you might be right there. It sounds great, but the process is never really so weightless – the best results are often hard-won. That is unjust somehow, but true. There is no gain really. But then when it happens those are moments of the luckiest chance.

RS: Are you fascinated by celebrity culture? And what about the effects you are producing yourself?

KL: Strumming the tune, banging the drum, is part of the job. That is truer than ever...OK, for me it is.

RS: In which type of society would you like to exist, ideally?
KL: I am satisfied with what is around me. It is our time and we deserve this time and the zeitgeist that comes with it.

Karl Lagerfeld stood up and straightened his necktie. It was time for bed. Reena's bad knee was throbbing. She was exhausted too. She had one more question, however:

RS: Can we expect yet another change of Style in the immediate future…?
KL: I let the doors stay open. Come what comes. What that is, nobody knows. I'm always ready. I don't really care: "It starts with me and will end with me!"

At which point, Karl Lagerfeld made a ceremonious exit, laughing and bowing, swinging his cane and strutting his way through the strangely deserted club.

What Reena really wanted to know was why – in a night club, for example – do we choose, always and above all, that nothing happens? Is it because this is how you can experience the delight of being everywhere and nowhere, of being there while being essentially elsewhere, preserving what we basically are to the point of never having existed?

There is a general context – Reena reflected as she hopped into a taxi – capitalism, Empire, whatever… there's a general context that not only controls each situation but, even worse, also tries to ensure that, most of the time, there is no situation. The streets and the houses, language and affects, and the global tempo that drives all of this, adjust themselves towards this sole effect. Everywhere, worlds have been arranged so they can slide over or ignore each other. The "normal situation" is this absence of situation.

That the desert of these times isn't perceived is only one more proof of the desert.

To live in the world means: to begin with the situation, not to deny it. To give consistency to a situation. To make it real, tangible. *Reality is not capitalist.*

Reena's cell phone was chirping in her pocket: Maris again.

Chapter 15

An imposing limousine, stretched to accommodate upwards of thirty people, and pulled by six black horses, was traveling down the west side of Central Park. The carriage was of a design that had become well known on the streets of the city after having been made popular through a music video. It consisted of a frame onto which had been dropped a series of four identical interlinking carved bodies. The repetition of these bodies was a deliberate attempt to streamline the vehicle and deliver the impression of a sumptuous and powerful volume. There were eight wheels and eight doors. The mudguards and supports were so overloaded with highly artistic carved ornaments that their technical function was barely discernible. The shell-shaped compartments appeared to float above the wildly turbulent ornamentation. Despite the proliferation of decoration, the vehicle was actually quite dynamic, its scalloped curves also part of what propelled it forward. It was stained black as the horses that pulled it, and along its sides were painted panels depicting Arcadian scenes from the four seasons. Clearly designed for joyriding, but unlike the optimistic décor of the new mass culture encountered in the city's great travel terminuses, this single stretched and encrusted vehicle suggested rather a terminal case of singularity, a kind of overgrowth of personality that left the pleasure principle that inspired it crippled and weak and in pain.

Wooden doors began to bang open and shut and feet hit the

pavements. Half-full glasses of liqueur smashed on the sidewalk, and as you expected a flock of bodyguards snaked out first before the limo discharged its more toxic, more potent contents proper, its genital material, its little beauties. The celebrities rubbed their eyes in the sun. Some were already wearing their shades. Their voices sounded thin and very far away.

"When I was small, I thought I was a horse," said Maris. She went over to one of the long black horses and patted its neck. Then she leaned her face towards the shiny coat as if scenting her young self. You could see she was really wasted. Meanwhile, Donald Trump, A-Rod, and Vincent Gallo were glowing beside her. They were wrapped in flag-like embroidered drapes, drinking beer on the street, and so drunk it looked as if they were a mass of alcohol holding itself together in the shape of men. Reena emerged last, the healthiest germ, spermatozoon, and started toward the park, pulling the others along in her wake.

Wow. This is it? The tent is tightly packed, with a stage inside and all kinds of banquet tables, tablecloths, flower arrangements, waiters (in the open-air cordoned-off backstage area), and hundreds of lolling spectators (in the front area). It is a National Cancer Society fundraiser involving the unveiling of two new public art-works and a live concert by The Strokes. Maris, the brains behind this event, provides Reena with an all-access pass, hangs the laminated card around her neck with her own excited hands. Both the park and the time are radiant and full. The trees' leaves overhead are turned jewel-like by the sun's rays and a massaging breeze. Even the squirrels are intoxicated, joyriding the branches of the trees. Joy joy enjoy yourself. Joy is the core of horror is joy. There is a whole scheme going on here. It is alive.

"Hello. How are you, Laser Girl?" Desire, light like spiders' webs.

Maris – in white dress and white flower for the hair, immaculate face – greets and chats with the various Cancer representatives, often posing in front of the banner for photographers and giving short statements to the roving TV crews. Reena is a picture too, a bit dazed by the too bright sun and a leafy, ballsy smell mixing with uptown perfumes and sweat. It all starts to happen. Cell growths? Ego growths. You bet!

"Thank you all for coming!"

Microphone feedback and the giddy, raspy voice of Maris draw the crowd's attention to a giant, guarded, veiled box on the Great Lawn. Cords are cut, champagne corks pop.

"Quand l'Institut d'…"

aaaaach…

A gust of wind rips the vinyl tarpaulin free and carries it across the park like a flying cartoon ghost. Laughter as it gets snagged in an elm in the distance.

"I ope zat you wheel fourgeev my purringleesh, butt I wood lyke two speek dearrectly wizzyoo. Zare cannes beano commune itay – an thees ees wat we arh ear four, no? – know commune itay bee tweanuz eef wee arh sep arated buy long weege. ok. Bon. Donc…."

A disheveled French dude is now addressing the crowd from atop an enormous, freshly assembled garage-like structure. The English Translator, stopped in his tracks, reverses, takes two steps back down: no way will he climb this thing.

"Zeese wurk ees ovcuss amposseeblegh wizzout urr partiseep-assion: zee four gottun meedil glassis. Ovcuss, sum wheel ownly sea zees struckture az a skullpture. Zare wheel be fotograves een mag-azeens of zeese construckshun an deesgushun ov aow eet wuz maid an aow eet ree laytes two my pree vyurs wurk. Nun ov zeese wheel shuhoh aow wee av kree eighted aye tempura airy or tonomuss zoan, annaow een zeese zoan, wee arull phree phrum ze rolls sosai-yeetay as preeskribed fourruhz. Pfeyenally eye sinksat twogezur wee wheel demmonstraight aow eet eese posseeblegh tuesskayp suhtch conpheinz. Az yuno, eet wuzwonov yoohoo caim upwizzee solooshun: you entair ear anpark ur veehickle. Zen you parse sroo ze deevaidink aria eentwo ze meedil zoan wear you wheel poot ur kah keese eentwo a bowelle. Een zeese meedil zoan, ucann 'angoot' weese udder partiseepants, aneet ze fude eyewheel pre-pair (sum lyte snaques andeeps). Wen you won toogo, utayke anne udder set ovkeese. Weese zeese keese you parse eentwo ze phinal aria ... wear, you wheel get eentwo aye deefair aint veehickle anne dryve a weigh phrum ur ohled lyve."

Reena feels the feeling of all-out exposure and it isn't just her. It's everybody exposing everything. All frills, all ferocity. How is it possible? There are little fires of hate and little fires of excitement. It is a high intensity mingling. She is happily shaken. Ecstatic for a moment. Then instant doom is setting in, dark spirits come out to play. Happiness feeds paranoia and vice versa. Sorrow laughs joy weeps. She sees upright braziers and men with goatees. buzz. Buzzzzz. Things, very untidy, damaged and unresolved. She sees her whole life laid out in front of her... she knows that she will collapse under the weight of her own ambitions that have never been expressed. Now she will save herself, she instantly says the magic words "I Is Had Gone" and all ambitions have zoomed out of her, forming an ethereal cloud over the tent. Reena matter. Discarded again.

It is already two hours into the event and the barriers are melting down. The VIP area and the semi-VIP area seem to become one united land of chat and socializing. The buffet-zones have been entered. Vertigo and thirst. Blubbery lips, naked brains and lusty bodies keep on oscillating. A roadie passes Maris a splif. Maris's voice is by now coarse and loud and she won't stop talking about The Strokes.

...the first time I saw a Stroke was at Amanda de Cadenat's birthday party. It was actually one of those groovy Hollywood parties where both Ione Skye and Mathew Perry were making the scene. It was at Keanu's mother's house though of course Keanu was off shooting the Matrixes. I was staring at this guy who looked like he was totally imitating Jeff MacDonald from Redd Kross's look circa their Montsano period, but he was prettier, rosy cheeked. Cherry-lipped, in fact. His clothes were also totally clean and new looking, creating an overall 'fresh' look. His Converses were so new that I felt deeply offended. Who does this guy think he is posing as a Ramone? As I so exclaimed to my friend, he said, "That's The Strokes' guitar player." Of course it was, how blind could I be (this was before I'd met Reena). It was like someone hit me over the head and into bizarro world. And there was the drummer hanging out with Drew. They make really good boyfriend-as-accessories, I have to say. The cute edge that doesn't threaten, more pink than black. That's how the nite started, very pink. My friend introduced me to the guitar player (can't remember his name). We started talking about NY, of course, both being NEW YORKERS… turns out he'd never heard of DNA the famous No Wave band that was a huge part of the 'cool NY scene' of the late '70s early '80s. He seemed very eager to learn, but my friend pulled me away mid-sentence and said, "Don't tell that asshole." Next he introduced me to Mathew Perry who said he loved my work. I thought that was the most insincere thing but I wasn't sure, or wanted to believe, so I told him I loved his work. But then thought that he must of thought I was totally full of shit to use a word like "work." Things were beginning to turn dark. I was beginning to feel too Hollywood and unclean. Time to go. The next time I met the jolly Strokes was at a Marc Jacobs show. They were very friendly and sweet. The one who looks a little like Billy Joel was swigging off a bottle of wine, didn't catch the label… true rock 'n roller, I guess. Bending reality has become the all-over occupation of the party. Everybody is playing. Nobody knows the game of tapping into the "noir universe". What happened to the glamorous, dark and truly charismatic shit. Does it exist? Did it ever?

Something about the pitch of her voice and the way her face is contorting is hurting Reena, as if when Maris spoke, it triggered inside her a torture instrument that crushed her organs. Reena says she'll be right back and, waiting in line at a bank of porta-potties, she meets, of all people, the Slovenian philosopher Slavoj Zizek.

Zizek is immediately charmed by gleaming, beaming Reena and has ditched his own dude-swarm entourage of academic types. The music is very loud so it's hard to hear all the words, but Reena is all ears as he tells her about his new book, *The Ghost Of Negation*. His sentences come like a continuous attack, deep rumbles of artillery shells, first from a distance, then progressively closer, but it is a benign fire. A search for truths. While he speaks there are fast successions of hand gestures, ticks, and his lips are wet from spit. Music starts blasting. Reena offers Zizek a powerbar. Balance, Detour, Yo-Bar, Zone in different colors. She could not help but pocket the whole range and put it in her purse. There was even a "will to powerbar" with the philosopher Nietzsche's head printed on the wrapping. She is truly excited to be able to offer this particular thing to Zizek. Massive fuel for the already massive machine. Zizek, in an all-gray flannel outfit – symbolizing some kind of phase in his life, serves as a most spectacular projection site and all possible spurts of thought need to be embraced. Reena seizes the moment and he loves the abuse, quite naturally.

Behind a group of ladies dressed in pastel colors, who after liquid and/or pharmaceutical breakfasts are now huddling in the brisk park afternoon, the second of the two public artworks is being unveiled. It resembles a mixture between a bus shelter and a romantic folly, while of course never offering any interior space that is not immediately visible from the outside – no junkie shoot-up shed, rapist dark alley, bum bedroom this – and waiting for the one possible redemption of some Brooks Brothers wearing kids burning it to the ground.

I can feel it all slipping through my hands, Maris was thinking as she ran her fingers through the bowl of roasted peanuts on the rock 'n roll offering table backstage. The Strokes were on stage, stroking it up. The table was laden with herbal ham, olives, carrot sticks, little puff-pastry pizzas, jellybeans, pickled chili peppers, all arranged in a mandala-like spiral pattern. Roasted peanuts are a dieter's nightmare, but what about unroasted peanuts in the shell? Minutes ago, Maris decided to give everything up, eliminate every-thing toxic about herself: stop cigarettes, stop alcohol, stop fat and fried foods, stop male fantasy, stop psychoanalysis, stop the over-extended and ambitious projects, and once again and always, to stop thinking about the outcome of situations. If I think about myself, this minute, I feel an enormous guilt about all the things that I am fucking up right now. My teeth are clenched, they should be relaxed. My boyfriend will arrive soon, and I wonder if he even is my boyfriend, does he want me that way, do I want him that way? I shouldn't care one way or the other when we're together. It just doesn't matter, and I should only matter in the way I am at any given moment. But I don't know who I am, what I am. I really want a cigarette.

Zizek was still Zizeking it up, saying that the drive is inherent-ly ethical, not "blind animal thriving" but an ethical compulsion which repeatedly compels us to mark the memory of a lost cause. The drive is the compulsion to revisit, to encircle again and again those sites of lost causes, of shattered and perverted dreams and hopes, not out of some nostalgic longing but because the marking of lost causes signals the impossibility of a totalizing morality, the necessity of a method called "ethical bricolage" that he borrowed from compadre-philosopher Laclau.

When Julian Casablanca opens his lopsidedly curled lip to sing, his voice doggie-paddling through the airy slush of soft kiddie guitar pop, all I can hear was him whispering in my ear. The occa-sional guitar jabs are not enough to disturb the dreaminess but eventually the shivers down my spine surprise me so much that I blush and look around to see if anyone noticed. Where is Reena? Central Park is confusing, so many different guards. Julian's resem-

blance to Roger, my teen crush is becoming a disturbing image.
They both have that english boy with slightly curled up girly hair
on the ends look, complete with milky pale skin and lips more
curled than mick jagger pouty. Roger was sixteen and I was fifteen.
He had a twin sister and they lived on nob hill in San Francisco.
We would take a little acid, just so we were all giggly and drive
around in their parents' Bentley. The Strokes were like mini rock-
stars, that's what made them appear so cute on stage, not that they
are small in size, only that because their music is small in scale, each
song like an 8mm movie backdrop for Julian's vocal: "ooh, ooh
yeh…" I can't really make out the lyrics but it doesn't matter
because I know they're all love songs to me… and I've been waiting so long for Roger to just hold my hand, I can't stand it, I've
never met a boy so shy, and gentle… the beginning and end of my
desire for the passive, evasive, boy. He can't move toward you only
out into the air… to open his mouth and sing. He grabs the pole
and drops off the stage into the audience… where is he? It's so dark.
Blue-black with just a spot of pink light searching in the crowd for
Julian. I look down at my pink stockings. Their shiny iridescence
makes my head swirl, and I suddenly feel sick to my stomach and
puke on some guy's shoes standing next to me. I panic and push my
way through the crowd. Inaccessible immensity, a hard-won state
of mind. I'm loving every minute of this.

Zizek knows that Maris doesn't care about cancer, doubts if she
even knows what it is, that it is the condition of one times one times
one always equaling one. What Maris knows is bringing one thing
into contact with another, one plus one. The Strokes and cancer.
Zizek and Reena. The cameras and the trees and the kids and cancer and chaos. One thing into contact with another. Cancer. A lot
of us have it, or will have it soon. Cancer, the condition of self
being referred to self, is hard at work today, and Maris is making it
work twice, three times. Bricolaging it.

Zizek brings his spitty lips close to Maris and begins to suggest radical changes in the structure of her company, Vive la Corpse. VLC should not pass up the opportunity to provide proof that it is our fantasies that support our sense of reality, that this is in turn a defense against the Real. The Real is the hidden/traumatic underside of our existence or sense of reality, whose disturbing effects are felt in strange and unexpected places: the Lacanian Sublime. He tells Maris she should figure out, with all her connections and her bricoleur's instinct, how to invoke this Sublime in ever more enigmatic ways. One elementary procedure could be moving forward from establishing shots of reality to a disturbing proximity that renders visible the disgusting substance of enjoyment, the crawling and glistening of indestructible life. And to combine this with new ways of invading daily existence. If the subject is a function of the difference between "subjective" pathologies and the libidinal economy of the "objective" ideological system, it must be precisely the gap between these two systems that founds the inherently split subjectivity. So, think about a company that grabs the leading edge in causing outbursts of the Real, with reality and its fantasmatic supplement acting side by side as though existing on the same surface. Reena Spaulings, you are this surface! You are the bricolage! Maris, Vive la Corpse is the perfect embodiment of difference. Work on the gap! Maris nods, a Yo-for-women powerbar clamped between her teeth like an old bone. She stares out into the crowd that has gathered around The Strokes and is terrified.

There is a person I imagine I want to be, someone different, different gestures, different reactions. I is had gone. Always thinking about death, my own, since I was nine years old. By now I should see it as a cheap fantasy: we die and then it's all over, good night, Irene. But what if death is a conversion into the most impossible, torturous beginning imaginable? You die, and are pressed into slavery to serve the will of some ruthless cosmic organism. Sure, maybe time and space don't exist anymore, but that's only to make you more efficient. All this means that human life on this planet is like some kind of vacation away from the gruelling prison of the universe. That explains all the steady over-population over the ages. We got wise and tried to make life as long as possible, and now word's getting around about how great it is here. All those souls crammed around the entrance, waiting for a uterus to take them through to the other side – either a middle-class jewel of existence worrying about getting a decent job to pay for all the comforts; or two weeks before being massacred with a machete in a jungle, anything, a floor scrubber, a pirate, a policeman, any form will do to forget, for awhile at least, the fluid formless coordination of the before and afterlife. That's why most people are terrified of dying. That's my fear of dying. When I look up at the stars, I see pure malevolence hiding behind the sheet of the atmosphere. Those simultaneous engines. Science wants to ruin everything, pull down the sheets and try to get the image a little clearer. The spirit of progress is a restraining device programmed at the genetic level, to keep us clamoring for something new, "the unknown," while deep down we know that we have become attached to this life and will suffer miserably to lose what's around us. I resolve to be more conservative. This moment has to last forever, and if it can't I will do something to freeze myself, begin to cry and never stop, retreat into the last reaches of my self and sew up the borders, so that no one will ever hear from me again. I need to ground myself. What if I ground myself on Zizek over there? What am I doing with my hands right now? One is on my hip and the other is holding a newly-lit cigarette. How'd that happen? Didn't I just throw my pack away? Zizek is standing right next to me, and he's putting away a cigarette case. So it was him. We've been having a conversation. Good, at least I'm not losing my mind.

Reena gets up and goes and sits behind an amp. Maris follows her though and starts crying on her shoulder, confessing her anxieties about soon having missed her chance to have a child, crying until all her tears are spent. Reena, crazily energized by her Zizek fix and a newfound sense of command over all this nothingness, cheers her up with her idea for a new project: a live riot, a musical, a Battle On Broadway, an untimely spectacle which she would like Maris to produce with underwear money. It will be called "Cinema of The Damned," and Reena will be its star. Maris prefers "Battle On Broadway." As The Strokes kick out their final jam, Jane feels another death drive coming on, and she will not go home tonight, not ever. Susan is deaf but can feel the song thudding repetitively against her eighteen year old flesh. Like a washing machine. Murielle is glad to be here and decides that New York can have her now, fuck Brussels, she's its. The Central Park event is ending. The crew of middle-aged white roadies in black jeans and band t-shirts start unplugging and winding the endless yards of electrical cords, packing up the equipment and amps and loading them into trucks. Reena's "bad idea" is floating there and refusing to go away, hooking into that part of Maris that makes her machine go, meshing with what she thinks of as her gears. She is emotionally spent and remains crumpled against Reena's shoulder, but in some part of her that never stops, she is working. Sensing the perfect moment, Reena convinces Maris to name her vice president of Vive la Corpse. The Strokes come backstage amidst a bustle of press, give a few interviews, drink a beer, and take off for their hotel. The Cancer people bid Maris and Reena goodbye with afterglow. Somehow Vive la Corpse had distributed some kind of monstrous but ungraspable desire all over the place, like walking sprinklers. And in the west the sun was setting.

* * *

Maris goes straight to the office without going home. She showers in the shower at the back of the janitor's office in the basement and begins to think about her thoughts. She's long since trained herself to do this when she knows she has to take a new direction. She's thinking about her thoughts. She outsources her desires. She likes to know people. She checks her brain while showering. She takes her mind's eye and quickly scans herself. Like you can do in the dark sometimes, when the edge of your mind is tired and there is a vacuum forming inside. Desires are outsourced and the vacuum remaining is massaged to provoke suitable responses to emotional stimulants. With a little concentration, the busy mind can train itself to check these responses. She was a quiet dark shape to herself for a moment. She saw shapes in there. They had drunk slivovice and taken some cocaine. She has the kind of willpower that can use stimulants as sedatives when she knows she needs to think. She settles the churning stimulated areas of her mind into curdled floating sections and begins to think. She puts certain parts of her brain to sleep with the party drugs and works on developing the professional presence of mind that allows her to think. She is perfectly aware of her molecular insufficiency and not in search of correcting it. At these moments, there is a deficiency of the organ-ic in her thinking. It is quite possible that she is thinking as if sheets of metal were communicating with each other inside her, between the curdled sections. A kind of futurist drawing, internalized. The excitement encapsulated by the party drugs is the chemical force providing her energy. She sees musicals made with people, like a kind of no-man's land of people that can be developed. She likes to know people, their intrigues and what they do. She thinks of musi-cals as a time-based space, a conveniently naked property that can be made more valuable to the investors by its additions. Then they sell it on at profit. The musical-riot in particular as a definition of property management. It is of no matter what they build on there. Except that certain formulas have to be made variable. Certain tra-ditional quotes and quirks are added. It is a traditional space. The local population is surveyed through the addition of your people. You add friends to the musical, people you manage, and through this, you control the reach of the riot. She lets her mind transform itself into the equivalent of some naked space in the former eastern bloc. She is a real estate representative looking at it. She sees the line of no-man's land reaching far ahead. There is much to do. It is not a revelation that she thinks about the *Cinema of the Damned* as a piece of property. It is the necessary construction that will allow her to move on. She does this systematically, without caring to make everything differently just because this time, things are new. She thinks very possibly of using not only Reena in the musical, she would like to add another actress from outside, an unknown. Experiment with making a Prada for Reena's Miu-Miu. This is good, because it means she can perhaps expand her business at the same time. Attract new clients. Women who need projects. Through her connections to restaurants and city zoning developments, she also knows of informal conglomerates, mostly men (she's good with men and also seems to know exactly when to sleep with them in the most natural and uncompromising way). Career men who are interested in ways of channeling and transferring money. She considers ways of getting money through future meetings with these men, commissions for other things she does, not necessarily always asking for money for this film project specifically. She sees tax deductions and the activation of hidden funds behind other names. Transfer of wealth. She sees meetings with journalists and magazine pages. The pages she imagines seem somehow brighter than before, in a kind of psychedelic way that can perhaps release their intrinsic decadences. This musical will chemically alter the consistency of the magazine's pages by refusing to sink into them. She also sees the intelligentsia she knows, the people who are diverted by her brightness, the people who like the way she widens her eyes and reveals her teeth and says something surprisingly pertinent in their dry world. They can help too.

She is interested in the work on this show because it reflects to her her parents and their cool and supportive upbringing, against which she could until now find no way to make a difference for

herself. She is also interested in the musical because working on it
and with it proposes a better way of managing her slight schizo-
phrenia than her perpetual edgy circling within the zones of accept-
ance does. Edgy circling within an outdated concept (her parents')
of what is good and worth fighting for. She is secretly ready for
some hideous exposure of her madness, instead of this refuge-as-
living that she has started to abhor. All of these thoughts start to
build up into a flame-fever, producing the feeling of self-induced
power. She has been excited by the people that she met that night
in a fresh way, beyond the belief systems inside of which she is used
to functioning. If she pauses for a moment, the effects of the drugs
and alcohol are nothing compared to the pounding insistence of
these people's presence. She recalls the other day, on the subway
between Spring and 14th Street, a huge crowd of black teenagers
entering the train, and the second they were on they start a screaming fight, on the brink of a physical fight between two girls. One
a girly girl the other one small, extremely well-groomed but like
a boy, and a supertough shouter. The noise in the car reaches
unbelievable ear piercing levels and the kids, all approximately
12–15 years old, standing on the seats, using the straps as swings
and making it totally impossible for anybody else to move. It has all
the ingredients of a very violent fight about to happen, and the
tough chick even amps it up by screaming: "gun-fight hhahhh?!"
An unbelievably cool and choreographed act that the whole group
is staging for the rest of the riders. Wasn't there a blueprint here
for what is possible? Maris sighs. This feels so good. Reasons to live
and living it and doing it are taking shape right in there in the
water. Maris sees her mind as one of those huge white octopussi
living in the deepest oceans. It is a most ardent environment,
but one that exactly causes the mind to live, even when no other
animal can do anything down there. A most transgressive, most
intelligent creature is down there. Those thinking eyeing tentacles.
Membranes. Sensors. Imagine: How to think like an octopus! Her

flesh starts to soften up under all that hot water showering.

Yes, she is still in the shower, where it is possible to think like this. She is taking her time, spinning out hair washing and perfunctory shaving. It is possible to think cleanly here, inside this old fashioned shower unit with its porcelain floor and institutional type fittings, with the smell of the mops hanging on the radiator. The futurist drawing inside her updates itself silently, and begins to become a bulleted list selected from a toolbar. The metal sheets dissolve into virtual bullets. Tightly.

She has to decide how to handle this piece of naked property that is the musical riot in such a way that it will not die. This is a basic paradox that has to become the material from which she will work. For the first time in her work on raising funds and support for projects, she is aware of a paradox. This is very exciting. She senses unconsciously the relationship between profit and a kind of deathly inevitability. She is going to be working between these states. She is vaguely aware that this is naïve of her, but she feels confident that she can play this card somehow. It doesn't matter. She gets out of the shower, uses the towel hanging there already (she is not hygiene obsessed, in fact, she can be very unaware of molecular boundaries sometimes), puts on her clothes again and takes the elevator. There is no one else around in the office yet, it is too early. She always has fresh clothes in the cupboard in the office. She writes herself a list.

- Get it off your desk, make it go away (she always writes that first)
- Timetable pitch – Allocations of Foundation funding?
- Millessima Database Access
- Oliver: who does he still need to make the Haydn Square project work. Get them.
- Dinner with Dominique and Michael and the children
- Reena Spaulingsnhnhj = Vice Prez.

Chapter 16

S he is getting there turning, flowing, failing, cunting, dancing, singing, shooting. You open fire, you open fire. All day long she prepares for the battle, singing: Youuuuuuu ooooopen fire fire fire.

Reena prepares. Forward somersault, finishing up on one leg. We practice standing, sleeping, walking (visible), walking (invisible), drinking a glass of water, screaming, kissing, vomiting, smiling, jumping out of a window, The Dance Number, swimming, fighting while swimming, dying, talking to a friend, talking to an enemy, the trapeze. "Tiger": spring forward followed immediately by a backward somersault. We need to get this thing off the ground.

What kind of body should I be?

Millions of bodies. It would seem that I should be able to say, to choose from the millions of bodies, the millions of lives I see about me, a body, a life that would please me.

Like Liz? Her body produces nice things. Lizzi is the state of energy combusting. A state of pleasure amidst energy flying, sparking, crackling.

She is a site, for things to take place. Even when she is alone she carries a whole mess of others with her, all around her. I like this. Characters are impressive. But they stand too distinctly. Their affects are still too individually packaged, there is a proprietorship to their aura and their actions, like Maris maybe. I always perceive a distinct line around their form. 'Lizzi' doesn't end with her form. She carries at least a hundred feet of space around with her. Space where a whole population resides.

Funny how individuality makes you generic. The lowest amount of body-ness belongs to this general realm of the individual self. All potential is abstractly relegated to the construct of a personal identity. All power is divested from the body. You can see. The 'body' is here just 'dumb' flesh – only meant to be pummeled into shape at the gym, to be dieted. The Self speaks, via identity, name, power, status, and the body is just a case for it. Model or not model. Almost model or not at all model. This is what the body has been reduced to. This and other impoverished inhabitations – like our idea of sex (Mr. Satisfied Coitus and Mrs. Erotic Orgasm) or on the dance floor on a Friday night. Maybe the face and the eyes are said to possess some 'mysterious' speaking capabilities, to offer chance 'views' onto the life inside. But there is a 'face' only where there is no body. Everyone looking out of their faces, but without bodies. They garnish themselves with lifestyles as a substitution for all the potentials of the body. But it's the materiality you are. And the material of your body is constituted by – more than your diet or your exercise program – your ideas, your practices, your desires. Your body is your response to the state of existing. Its material should have a very singular texture... taste... presence, consistency, set of affects...

Reena sits back and waits for her toenails to dry.

Like Jutta. Obviously from some tough intellectual stance adopted long ago, she has learned certain ways of avoiding the pitfalls of a 'self.' She has made her body an Artist, an expression machine, constituted it on Interests. You can see that she has devoured tirelessly, inhumanly, way into the nights, the whole avant-garde corpus. Books, ideas, movements, figures, photos, data, other lives. I can almost tell the place on her body where she has digested Artaud, Rimbaud. Hers is an intellectual body of pure capability, but one that is also open, looking to be determined from outside, ready to re-write everything, to co-write, to be written on... feature for any Now... co-efficient of glamour... faceless avant-garde.

And Stefan. Body of tears, trips, bruises, and sudden elations. A travelling, fumbling, tumbling body. Stefan is always being produced, by where his body is going, what it comes into contact with, what happens to it. A continuous process. A body that doesn't know to protect itself, but is really just a 'body' – travelling, feeling, expressive. And he emits a continuous flow of speech of everything he is experiencing, to everyone present, familiar or stranger alike. He is the script of his travelling body. He has no clue about privatizing these matters. And he's right. They are beautiful when they're out there.

Reena imagines herself a single blaze composed of those three bodies, a super-flame. She tries translating the blaze-thought into a blaze-walk-question, a walk that is asking how to do it. Once your walk becomes a question, it's hard to go back to when it was a poorly concealed fact, a fact that was only concealed from itself. She notices three Wall Street guys walking together, jacketless, each of their right shoulders lower than their left.

Reena prepares ghost images of herself, by layering thought, like paint, making juxtapositions of tone and color, staking out some kind of opaque territory. Opaque like the sidewalks.

Eating lunch with Maris: We only go to one restaurant for lunch anymore, it's called the 'Rendez-vous.' Sometimes we invite friends to join us and we enter the restaurant together. We take lunch at a measured pace – there's no reason to hurry. We look up and out of the window. We listen to the pleasant din of the lunchtime restaurant as if from a distance. We lean back slightly when the food is brought to us, to make room for the plate, and if we are with company, we break eye contact at this point. We eat more carefully than we do at other times of the day. We don't put too much on our fork. We don't look up from our food very often. We use lunch to endow the rest of our day with precision.

Sing your name… Joseph. Sing Joseph. Evoke this Joseph. Who is he, this stranger? Go on singing your name – Joseph – asking: Joseph, who are you? What are you? Find the mask of Joseph's face. Is this really Joseph's mask? Yes, this is the essential Joseph. And now it is this essential Joseph, his mask, that sings. We notice that our voice changes, deepens, and becomes unrecognizable.

Stand with your feet flat on the floor and about shoulder width apart (toes slightly turned out), keep the abdominals tight and the lower back in a neutral position. Slowly descend until the upper legs are parallel to the floor – using a back and down movement (as if you were sitting into a chair). Then push back up to the starting position.

Reena prepares herself by being pathetically stuck for a couple of days. Re-learning the drift. She prepares herself as a something signifying something. She met a man on the subway platform who was asking "How do I get to the F?" It was clearly marked on the signs and the man was pointing to the signs. "I'm upside-down I just had surgery on my eyes." He needed to know how to walk towards the sign, how to go up the stairs (which for him was down), and so on. Reena followed behind him, his disciple for five minutes.

In the revolving bar on top of the Marriott Marquis hotel in midtown, we run through the "battle" variations. Jef is showing us the way we walk through a choreographed brawl and order a glass of water at the bar. Start walking slowly, as if with great difficulty and effort. Suddenly, after standing still for a moment, start to run very lightly and gracefully. This is how we dance through a disaster, taking its energy and its chaos with us and into the water. This is how we drink water in the new city with our new mouth. Another example: The blossoming and withering of the body. In the second phase, the limbs-branches wither and die one by one. "I feel like a million bucks." Say it with the mouth, with all of our

mouths. Choose an emotional impulse (such as crying) and transfer it to a particular part of the body – a foot, for example – which
then has to give it expression. A concrete example of this is Eleonor
Duse who, without using her face or arms, "kissed" with her whole
body. Express two contrasting impulses with two different parts of
the body: the hands laugh while the feet cry. The abdomen exults.
A knee is greedy. "I feel like a million bucks."

When Jesus got out of the boat a crazy man with an evil spirit
came from out of the graveyard to meet him. This man lived in the
graveyard and no one could keep him tied up anymore, not even
with chains. The man shouted at the top of his voice what do you
want with me Jesus son of the most high God, Swear to God that
you won't torture me! (Because Jesus had said to him, come out of
this man you evil spirit.) And Jesus said what's your name. Legion.
My name is Legion because we are many. And he begged Jesus
again and again not to send them away. Reena loved how Legion
went from I to he to we to he to them, and she desired it, that is she
began to require it. There was a large herd of pigs milling around
on a nearby hillside, eating. The demons begged Jesus, send us
over to the pigs and let us to go into them. Jesus agreed to that and
the evil spirits came out of the man and went into the pigs. The
herd about two thousand in number rushed down the steep bank
into the lake and were drowned.

She prepares making her already complex relations with people
around here even more complicated. Improvisation in all areas.
How to change a woman in an instant. How to be nothing but a
negotiating machine, a lubricating jelly, how to slip. Even the
quantum physics people who apply quantum physics to "your life"
seem to believe so much in the self. The personal spirit. "The ghost
in the machine." Why do people making discoveries about this self
always have to be sitting on a sofa with a giant cup of coffee, a
jumbo-tasse, in a house or loft with hardwood floors? Don't be
so hateful.

How embarrassing it is to drink orange juice, the juice of self. Better to eat candy like Andy. How compromising it is to use toilet paper, the paper provided for the self, and to always be wiping one's ass. "My" ass. That whole idea. Like voting. Sacrosanct. Very personal. Very *one*. (Don't be hateful). How mortifying it is to be embarrassed! To be one, a singleton. Better to be a simpleton (less than one), or more than one (Legion), but not one. Be zero, a true hole (*trou*), a place holder.

Reena prepares herself for being a cathartic piece of work, a desire-releaser, an I-love-you.

How regrettable when people all around the world start becoming selves, tooth-brushing, anus-wiping, voting selves, Americans. I guess it has to happen before anything else can happen?

Things You Can Do to Change: To make yourself taller, two or two and a half inches can be quickly added to your height by tearing or folding a newspaper to form a ramp in the heels of your shoes. If you are wearing high top shoes, even more can be added. Be certain that you relace them tightly and tie a double knot. Such ramps have an added advantage in that they also change your walk and posture. Hoist your trousers up and tighten the belt. This will make your legs look longer.

Try the old trick of buttoning your pants to your vest to acquire a stoop. Basically, posture and gait must fit the type of person you are portraying, his age, upbringing, physical condition, degree of ambition, and his whole outlook on life. One section of the crowd will move with a purpose, preoccupied with their own important little lives. Another group will slouch or waddle along, like dully curious animals. Any little object catches their interest for a fleeting moment. They have no goal in life and every movement and line of their body shows it. Be sure your face has that drooped, dull, set expression of one who has had a stroke. The eyes are usually all that move, with a bewildered, anxious expression as though the person does not quite know what has happened to him. A small stone or other hard object (a detachable pencil eraser, for example) in one sock heel will produce a convincing limp. Slightly larger ones in the arch of each foot will produce a "flat foot" walk. The last-mentioned device also aids in maintaining an "old age" gait.

More Quick Changes: A good swarthy skin color can be had by wetting your hands and rubbing them on an old piece of rusty iron. The fume-vent of a water heater is usually a good place to find it. A mechanic's face can be effected by rubbing in black grease from an engine or hubcap, and then rubbing some of it off. Shoeblack rubbed very thin on the face gives a gray, unhealthy, almost dead look to the skin.

We imitate natural sounds and mechanical noises: the dripping of water, the humming of a motor, etc. Then fit them into a spoken text. We should develop the ability to speak in registers that are not our natural ones – i.e. higher or lower than normal. The basic rule for good diction is to expire the vowels and "chew" the consonants. The ability to handle sentences is important and necessary. The sentence is an integral unit, emotional and logical, that can be sustained by a single expiratory and melodic wave. Learn this, then unlearn it.

She started reading *Nine Years Among the Indians* by an ex-German boy, Hermann Lehmann, who was kidnapped by Apaches down in Texas.

Reena prepares speaking German to people who cannot understand German.

The boy was kidnapped along with his younger brother. They were immediately exposed to treatment that appeared to be torture, while being kept constantly on the move. The younger brother escaped the day after they were captured. Hermann had a chance to escape too, but actually exerted himself to rejoin his captors, who rewarded him with more intense "torture." They made him spend that night suspended by the arms and legs, face-down, blacked-out, with two heavy stones on his back. Seven years later he had to leave the Apaches after murdering the medicine man who had killed his original captor, Carnoviste, whom Hermann loved. Rather than rejoin his Texas family he wandered around in the desert for a year, then became a Commanche.

The Indians were cowards, and whenever there was danger they would send me. The first horse I tried to steal was a large black mare staked near Fort Concho. The Indians were afraid to go up to him, for they thought somebody was watching. Carnoviste told me to go for the horse. I hesitated. He drew his gun and commanded me to go, and of course I consented – a boy can't answer such an argument. He gave me a pistol and I moved cautiously toward the horse, crawling part of the way. I saw something bulky near the horse and thought I could see it move. I was within three feet of the bulk. I cut the rope that held the horse, when suddenly the man (for it was a man) rose up and shot at me. Reena loved how the objects, animals and people were trans-entities. The charge passed just over my head, but the smoke and fire blinded my eyes and made me deaf in one ear for a month. I was so excited that I dropped my pistol and forgot to get it in my haste to get away from there. The noise and confusion stampeded the horse, and I think the man must have run, too. I ran a short distance and hid in the high grass and lay still for a long time. After a while I heard wolves howling and went to them, not wolves, but my companions, for that was our signal when we were separated. I told the Indians that the pistol was shot out of my hand, and that it fell in reach of the white man. Had I told the truth I would have had to have gone back for the precious weapon.

When you are finished, take a moment to relocate your self.

A Dance Number: We have this big full-length mirror in one of the bedrooms. It is a long thin thing and you can only see one person at a time. Maris doesn't want us to dress the same. We jig about clicking our fingers, moving backwards and forwards. We argue a lot with Maris, this gives our numbers a fresh feeling, and our fights blow over quickly. One minute one of us is storming out of the room, the next we're all back inside, working harder than ever.

We work on our resonators.

a) The upper or head resonator which is the one most employed in European theatre. Technically, it functions through the pressure of the flow of air into the front part of our head. We can easily become aware of this resonator by placing the hand on the upper part of the forehead and enunciating the consonant "m."

b) The chest resonator, known in Europe although rarely used consciously. To use it, we speak as though the mouth were situated in our chest.

c) The nasal resonator which is also known in Europe. It has been unjustly abolished by most theatre schools.

d) The laryngeal resonator, used in oriental and African theatre. The sound produced recalls the roaring of wild animals. It is also characteristic of some jazz singers (e.g. Armstrong).

e) The occipital resonator. This can be attained by speaking in a very high register. This resonator is commonly used in classical Chinese theatre.

f) In addition, there exists a series of resonators which we often use unconsciously. For example, in so-called "intimate" acting, the maxillary resonator (in the back of the jaws) comes into use. Other resonators are to be found in our abdomen and in the central and lower parts of our spine.

g) The most fruitful possibility lies in the use of our entire body as a resonator. A total resonator.

Vomiting: When we vomit, we go through several stages. We begin by slowly responding to the swells of nausea in our stomachs. We have to take our time over this, it should be a similar process to putting off a treat. We are apprehensive and sad and bored all at once. We make sure to wait until there is no doubt that we have to vomit. Then we shift our position and have to run. The first stage of vomiting involves taste and the regurgitation of things we might remember having eaten and drunk. These things have a strong acid burn. It's not possible to think very much while vomiting at this point, there is a lot of stuff coming out and it takes up most of the time. The terrible headache we have is magically suspended for the duration of the vomiting. When we stand up from vomiting, the headache will return with a sharp blinding stab on the left side of our skull. We rinse out our mouth and keep spitting until the long unbreakable chain of saliva left behind after the vomit is finally expelled. This is usually quite difficult. We vomit every few hours, sometimes two or three times in one hour. New movements or smells can induce another bout of retching. Soon, there is only the water we have been sipping left to vomit up. As the substances we expel get thinner and thinner, it becomes possible to think more and more while vomiting. The temporary suspension of the otherwise perpetual headache allows for a range of extraordinary thoughts to enter the mind. Occasionally, as specks of yellow bile are catapulted into the porcelain bowl, we catch ourselves in these thoughts, but only for a moment. They can continue for the most part uninterrupted, as in a magic spell. We get emptier and emptier. Colors we have never seen before come out of us – yellows and greens and flecks of red. After around 8 hours of this, the hunger slowly begins. We have to time how to treat this hunger quite carefully, and not sate it too soon. Nibbling Rich Teas and sipping herbal infusions, we can begin to return to the world. The thing is, we have never loved the world so much as at these moments that we are restored to it. When we can walk again, and eat the biscuits without throwing them up, and talk to the man in the shop once more, we go outside into the evening sunshine and walk in the flat dry park at the back of the house and the evening is really, at last, very beautiful. Everything is fresh, we have no problem liking the people we see, and nothing is dramatized.

Meditating before a burning car Reena considers things one can do to change: It will be much easier to switch from a bank clerk to a tramp, for example, than vice versa. Consider also the district you have to pass through. If it is the wharves, you will be less noticeable as a seaman, a truck driver or a stevedore. If it is a financial district, become the most typical of clerks. You will find that one idea will suggest another. If possible, get into your complete cover clothes, stand before a mirror, study every detail of your appearance and ask yourself, "What can I do most quickly to change that person?" Reena stole an issue of *Self* magazine from a newsstand, and was sent (by the mother of a friend) a copy of *The Potent Self* by Moshe Feldenkrais. The importance of "props" or accessories should be mentioned again. Certain props definitely reflect a man's personality, and for our purpose can help give him a personality. This is particularly true of smoking. Different types of cigarettes and the many ways of handling them are a surprisingly good key to their user. Briefcases, bundles and their wrappings, lodge pins, rings, even lapel flowers, all have their personality and will help add to yours. Sometimes, too, they serve to attract the eye to the extent that you, personally, are not scrutinized. How many times have you read descriptions in the paper where a witness says, "Well, he had a red flower in his button hole, and I think a sort of greyish suit, but I'm not sure." The flower had caught the eye to the exclusion of all else.

She hosted a number of arguments, wars, congresses, liaisons, boredoms, panics, picnics, in the space that might have been referred to as her self, our self.

One of the most assuredly human things is to be a conversant and conductive body in social interaction. Instead, be a rug. Develop the rug-like capacities of your speech, your expression, of how you position yourself between the others at social gatherings. Become an impasse, impassively absorbing without signification. As a rug absorbs spills, odours and dirt, becoming more and more pregnant. Practice embodying a sociability breakdown. Along all the communication networks, relays, highways, see if you can create confusion, traffic jams. Pile-ups and accidents. Be only your matter – opacity, density, weight – but an opacity, density and weight more alive than their liveliness! and more communicative than their communication!!

She deliberately gave herself food poisoning and experimental hair extensions. A change of hair style is one of the most simple and effective aids in changing a woman's appearance. The position of the part should be altered or eliminated altogether. If the hair is usually worn closely set, brushing it out frizzy and adding a ribbon bow will create a different effect immediately. The advisability of taking along extra hair to use as a braid should be considered. The style chosen should be one that a woman can arrange herself, naturally, without recourse to a beauty parlor. An important point to remember is that the most unbecoming hair style will probably change the wearer's appearance more than any other. If a woman does not want to be noticed, she should strive to look mousy or old or dumpy. If the work calls for glamour, an expert on make-up should be consulted. Reena began to use language differently.

We considered our "mind" to be a foot... on whose leg? And our first taste of madness to be a very roomy shoe. Our strategy was to lose your connection with our "roots" by moving – not away from them, but wherever she could see to go. Reverse lunges. Donkey Kick: start on all fours, keep back flat. Breathe out and push leg straight out behind you, bring knee back to chest and repeat. Change to other leg.

She monitored the extent to which we avoided "danger." She studies and steals from the most unlikely objects, from forgotten worlds, stories: Richard Dadd's fairy paintings. In these 19th century paintings you can see pitched battles between armies of fairies over the territory of a tuft of grass near a tree root.

Meeting a friend at a station. When we meet Maris at the station, we keep it in mind all day. The train has a time of arrival that we keep making ourselves remember. We travel to the station in good time wearing clean clothes. We take a book with us and buy a newspaper on the way. We feel small in the station, and check the arrivals board. We find out the platform number and go there, even though it is still at least 15 minutes before this particular train is due. This is just simply to make a physical check on the platform. We drift off again. We lean against a pillar to wait, rather than sit miles away. In this mood, we think about how to treat our friend and her concerns when she arrives. We keep an eye on the gap where the passengers come through off the trains. We see her approaching the barrier and we walk towards it ourself as well. She raises a hand and we wave back. Without saying anything, we make our mouths say hello. She hands her suitcase over the barrier to us and we take it, then she comes through herself. We kiss her by leaning towards her, our mouths are open because we were about to speak, then we re-direct our lips away from the words and push them forward instead. By touching her cheek with them, we can make a slight pressure on her skin, before pulling away again. We are aware that she might be doing the same thing to our cheek too. The way she smells suddenly becomes close to us and then pulls away again. We walk through the concourse together. A quick change: If you have a pair of glasses and were not wearing them before, put them on.

The body is just one part of a 'body.' Our expression organ isn't necessarily on our body. Nor our sexual organ. Coming up, an experimentation that definitively shatters the performer-spectator model. People want to be someones. But the really exciting challenge is to become no one. And where will you find no ones? In nowhere. Where things are exploding.

Chapter 17

F OR IMMEDIATE RELEASE: There is no such thing as death. Death only exists because you are afraid of it. You are afraid that death is negative entertainment, or none at all. Or is it the ultimate diversion, the other side of the screen, a dazzling extra-tainment? What happens when the body dies? Imagine how confusing it must be to be taken away from everything that you have known. When your body dies, you are simply, out of your body. There are no rules out of the body. Play with other people's bodies. For more info: (212) VIV-ELAC.

FOR IMMEDIATE RELEASE: What is Vive la Corpse!? At times capable, incapable, fumbling, agile, interested, uninterested, disin-terested. How to describe the art of turning away from art through fashion, and then the turning away from the underwear business through experimental cinema, through a Battle On Broadway? No longer a corporation, Vive la Corpse is a "name-used-in-common" or a "blank signature." The only reason the word 'corporation' still applies is to evoke the particular legal and fiscal entity which enjoys a different authority than that of the individual acting alone. (212) VIV-ELAC.

Every day it will happen. "I call it the 'tense hour.' It starts around twelve o' clock." *L'heure tendue.*

Around noon, the winds would blow in coldly from under the left frontal lobe of the brain and then Maris would feel that whatever she was doing at that moment was artificial. If she was looking at her planner to see what appointments to keep and phone calls to make in the afternoon ahead, she would feel the artifice of the paper caught in the binder's rings, held by the leather cover that was her guiding book in this hour.

"I keep pretending like I'm doing something, and I don't know why, so I pretend to do it anyway to make one part of my brain happy."

As well, there was the strangeness of gravity that she would feel with her ass in a chair. When her hand moved the mouse to glide the pointer over the Inbox of her email program, she would feel the strain of cartilage groaning in mid-evolutionary spasms.

"It starts slowly, with conflicting expectations, and in their conflict it seems they cannot be fulfilled."

She called out to instinct in that hour and instinct, buried so remotely, would never call back. She would walk around the block, looking for old buildings, just to touch their stones. And she would touch those stones, for the ages, while a week's worth of stale urine nearly knocked her out. She would go to Washington Square to find a tree to hug. And she would hug a tree in an arabesque pose, to avoid stepping in the dried dogshit.

"Me wanting to concentrate and it not happening. Noon. It's not happening. It's a tug of war. It can start with big ideas that aren't fulfilled and then it fragments into little ideas."

Meanwhile, the clients would never stop calling. They entrusted her completely and to conceal that fact in light of the invoice due to be addressed from her office, they never trusted her. It was the Front that they kept and she maintained, so that, with every application of the airbrush to Reena's scanned and digitized breasts, there had to be a conference about, what were the other possibilities? Can they glow more? Can they be less elastic? Is that yellowish mole under the left one a statement or not?

"The thoughts are in my head and I won't realize it's happening and then it's too late and I can feel it instead in my body. The blood in my brain is boiling, gets really tense. This is not a metaphor. Certain points of my spine give off cotton electricity. My veins hurt as well."

FOR IMMEDIATE RELEASE: anxiety, insomnia, headache, sweating, sneezing, wheezing, blurred vision, hot flashes, distraction, abnormal breathing, abnormal thinking, abnormal dreaming, abnormal gait, dysphonia, aphasia, amnesia, coma, nervousness, dizziness, impaired concentration, chills, malaise...

There was a certain light of twelve o' clock Maris remembered from when she was thirteen. Dead-on high, shadows and brightness, vertical scaling, heaven and hell. Never take snapshots of loved ones at that moment of chaos and confusion. Judgment Day with an angel trying to haul a corpse out of the grave by the hand, while a cross-eyed demon with fangs in the stomach gnaws at the foot.

"And then I start to go over everything, again and again, how to get out of it, what I could do. This makes me go into a frenzy, a panic."

She never had sex at that hour, was always careful to avoid it, but that didn't stop her from ruminating about what she was missing. Giving a blow job could be like sucking a jolly and vital root, and then a second later it could be just a dick in the mouth. A thumb in her ass brings her into her self, she would reason, and in the tense hour she would miss that thumb sorely.

"The thoughts start to loop slowly. Sometimes other people are in my head, telling me how they would do it. And then I think about it. About my incapacity."

The struggle of improvisation would be waged minute by minute. Improvising as terrible acting, the robot unplugged from the central command structure.

"It's always being cut off, because it's not thought through, not lived out, and I have to start over again."

One can get rid of a great many things, yet one does not get rid of them all. The corpse of your leg is what you get if you free your leg from your trunk. "What am I?"

FOR IMMEDIATE RELEASE: You have not seen me in a while. I started to withdraw already a while ago. I could not figure out what was happening. I never really did. Well, there were a lot of good things going on. I wasn't free enough, I would not get drunk with you. I could not be in your crowds. All my nocturnal desires went into the accumulating darkness of dead endings. I'm a poor substitute for a person, scenester, artist, whatever. I wanted to be a friend.

All my life I believed in the perceptions, that through a direct excitation of the appropriate neuronal centers, by means of drugs or electrical impulses, situations get changed. I always thought that whatever kind of chemistry went on in my body and in my brain, it was producing a drug that opened new dimensions of shapes, colors, smells for me. Fantastic assaults. But there was no connection. I kept going and going on. I invented all kinds of symptoms, fabricated all kinds of dreams. Well, it had to do with you and it had nothing to do with you. It had it all. The sole reason was to invent disturbing, creepy, adventurous, sometimes stylish life, and product for you.

There was the comic horror of the fundamental fantasy, the idea of love, and then there was the fact that this life is an ongoing sequence of violence real and imagined that gets equalized, stretched out by the everyday business and by the pain, and I do feel these moments. I'm trying to use some words and some images to illuminate the world. I feel like it's failing almost all the time.

Fundamental, and that was what you showed me so well is the ugliness of it all. Of us, of what we do, history. Turning more dissonant. Burning up. Confusing times. But then, what the hell with my me? I will be there. I'll be at your side, at one or four, or so. To tell you stories of self-inventions and self-destructions, of de-selfings. In all my cries and groans, my imagined and my real and profound emotional isolation, my perseverances, breakthroughs and breakdowns, I'm part of you. You have not seen me lately. I'm not sure of my reappearance but perhaps you'll find me there in a truly new decompositional matter.

It was noon in the office and the intermittent hum pause hum of press releases going out was a calming music to Maris, who couldn't help worrying about the situation up here. Reena was inviting all these new things, people, bodies and notions into the office. Plenty of shady and hairy types too. Maris would have liked to have seen where it was coming from, or even just to feel that Reena saw where it was coming from. Maris was good at taking bets on where things might go, but she couldn't get her distance on this one. And Reena seemed to only ever see by not seeing. The Apparent was, to Reena, only a bunch of obstacles thrown in the way, catching or blocking the light like a screen, and she was always very dissatisfied until she could find a way into that running stream of darkness through which light could pass unnoticed, unimpeded, unchecked.

FOR IMMEDIATE RELEASE: Members of C.R.A.K. (CAPI-TAL REJECTS, ALWAYS KICKASS) will be previewing their gang walk on Broadway next Saturday night. Eyewitnesses can expect to see "Stinky" Solomon, Charlie Mako, and Jef Martinet doing the demonstration. Their cover will be as hoodlums promoting the upcoming song-and-dance riot "Cinema of The Damned" – and FXtreme-box. They'll be driving by in a ruby minivan airbrushed with characters from the game and blasting the Bowl-Cream Progeny exclusive soundtrack. Aside from putting up promotional signage, distributing T-shirts to the hungry, unloading boxes of demo CDs, and pressing bumper stickers into eager fists, they will also be cutting holes in coat pockets, getting some red ink on some faces, molesting certain cops, spitting on windshields, selling actual fake diet pills and other such nonsense in order to show off their latest ambulatory exercise.

12:01 – vibrations from bottles rattling on the table, a serving cart. 12:09 – saliva tasting like copper. 12:11 – praying for a moment of soothing blankness. 12:17 – one is born as an individual and then gets a personality. 12:22 – slipping and falling into the river, attacked by rusty tin cans. 12:39 – being pushed face first through revolving doors. 12:40 – what organizes all the colors in a shop window is what punctures my resistance. 12:46 – running for no reason except to put out a fire. 12:55 – waiting for planes to crash.

Running from one store to the next, looking for something perfect, but getting nothing because nothing is perfect.

"I feel I'm fake. Not my actions. Losing my center. Going around the possibilities of my self."

FOR IMMEDIATE RELEASE: Needing at least three people to pull it off, the C.R.A.K. walk is a veritable ballet of thigh-rising hilarity and outright terrorism. The point man leads the center with a gentle crooked lope, chin tucked in, shoulders strung high, and hip jutting out stiffly. His incline is at an angle, leaning forward, so that it seems as if he is climbing a sand dune, or that his head is an engine dragging dead weight held up by the legs. Instinctively, you want to jump out of the way for fear of having him fall forward into you, a headlong stumble. Flanking right and left are "the sidewindlers," the ones who make this walk what it is. With no particular style or visible ticks, theirs is a simple back and forth motion, fanning out and closing in, speeding up and slowing down, all the while being led inevitably forward by the sensational gait of the point man. Unwitting victims get trapped, become the fondled or fondlers, muggers or mugged, beaters and/or beaten in this walk that acts like a kind of three-pronged pedestrian thresher, even a high-science, selective tunafish net.

Up in the offices of Vive la Corpse, there was a growing feeling that the culminating point of time had been discovered, where time burned with more heat than elsewhere, and would never suffice, where one heard the "roar of the cataract of time" as well as time's winged chariot drawing near, and declaimed, "never again will we drink so young!"

It is three o'clock in the afternoon. Reena is sitting at her new desk. A Formica rectangular supported by four hollow aluminum legs. The only thing on it is a bowl of duck noodle soup, and Reena is waiting for it to cool down a bit so she can eat some. She fishes out a fatty slice of duck and holds it in the air for twenty seconds, blows, waits a few more seconds, then takes it slowly into her mouth. Chewing, she watches the hands make their slow, calm sweep of the clock's round face and, turning her attention to what else there is to see, admires a yawning Maris's seemingly unconscious abilities with the fax machine at the other desk.

FOR IMMEDIATE RELEASE: "Stinky" Solomon always does things in a de-centered way. He cuts the grain so that all the lines go askew skidaroo. His latest thing is murderous property scams in the Catskills lined up with notaries, meat grinders, quicklime, sledgehammers, and ravines. But to really notice his art, you have to wander into Stinky's daily life. The guy has process written all over him. He removes the claws of cats for spare change. He's the first one to unfurl banners that say, "Shit is shit!" He'll tape up the boundaries we all take for granted and charge double for admission.

Charlie Mako is a suicide specialist. With him, wasting things is a delicate pastime. How many pockets slowly unthreaded? How much make-up smudged? Poor Charlie, genius-in-waiting, cares nothing for his friends, his loves, his enemies... but he does have a penchant for pointless arguments that he chooses with passion. Great for diversions, Charlie will always cause a scene at the worst moment and then sacrifice himself for the good clean getaway of everyone else.

Jef Martinet can conceal anything on his body. He could be stark naked and still surprise you with a bouquet of roses. A dinner jacket might be lined with stainless steel knitting needles. Earrings with hashish. Packs of cigarettes with razor blades. A sun hat hides a disassembled box-cutter. A striped necktie, sacks of cocaine. Jef often forgets where he hides things, just like any great inventor or squirrel. With a surveyor's eye for clothes and objects, he captures the weak link in any system so even repression and laws become places from which to carve out new weapons.

It is a large, airy office on the 19th floor of a glass tower, with spacey views of other towers and, between these, a section of the Hudson River and New Jersey in the distance. Reena likes the low-pile wall-to-wall carpeting, the views, the empty spaces between the uncluttered desks, the vacant leather couch, the air hockey table that no one ever used. Mostly she likes the eventlessness of this office, and figures that any real office today works by sealing itself off from whatever it creates, producing a sort of vacuum from which sparks – faxes, phone calls – could be produced and transmitted. It was first of all a question of emptying out the space behind the company logo, which functions as a sort of mask or fog bank behind which anything at all, or nothing, could take place, or not. Vive la Corpse was a particularly opaque face, and slipping behind it now to feel the length and width of a full workday at company head-quarters is a rich experience for her. She feels perfectly at ease in her new role as Vice President. There is nothing going on here. Just lunch. And the grinding hum of the press releases going out. There is also Henry Codax, the bearded, taciturn painter to whom Maris rented out the Northeast corner of the office. Codax thrived in this particular light. He works silently and without pause. He is a radical painter in the old school sense, and devotes his practice to a steady production of expensive, intimidating monochromes. He has mastered what kind of work not to do, the difference between right and wrong work, and is coasting, masterfully. Reena watches him rolling a coat of bubblegum-pink semi-gloss enamel across a large canvas in the corner. He has spread out plastic tarps to protect the carpet. He wears a paint-splattered pair of overalls and no shirt, plus paint-encrusted Timberlands, and smokes a pipe. At his feet, among the tubes of paint and turpentine-soaked rags, was a half-drunk bottle of Remy VSOP and a boombox. The Rolling Stones record *Emotional Rescue* is playing softly. He has it on repeat. *Heaven*.

The fax machine is still making its music again. In an office, stuff doesn't just go out, it comes back in. Just as Maris hoped, her tray begins to fill with hate mail and counter-releases, a sure sign that the world is listening, that their transmissions were finding homes abroad, fields of hairy tendrils and stems that they, like butterflies, were tickling into life, into a breezy wakefulness. Paris always resented Maris, who skims a fax from an ex-employee there before pinning it to the wall in the hall.

FOR IMMEDIATE RELEASE: Everything emblematic of a being-alive that once was, is now available in a variety of prices and quality. The orders are placed, sales are calculated and rectified, magazines go to print, shop lights go on and off. And everyone rejoices that signs of difference and intensity are now being found on every body and in multiple walks of life – never questioning the vitality of these signs. You have rid yourself of danger, excitement, glamour, the pursuit of life, the possibility of life itself even. They were too costly and ungainly, too threatening and consumer un-friendly. Who has remained are the entourage, the hangers on, the behind the scenes toilers. These are your stars these days – and they act every bit the star, with their attitudes and their cell phones... You are a city of petty-créateurs – the art director, the model booker, the PR agent, the restaurant owner... It's no wonder that there exists in you a foul strain of snobbery, which is experienced at its height of foulness and senselessness in the 'employee of the trendy used designer-clothing boutique.' If you could imbue a DKNY dress with human-like capacities, this is who it would be. Born of a race of products, she speaks the language of the marketplace, without a trace of human warmth or dimension. She is the deputy of a fascism of the non-living. (Ouch!... —mp)

Here in Paris, where I've been for only a month, I would not jump to any conclusions of it being a more inhabitable city. I do however like how its bodies don't shelter themselves from the rain, how a chocolate truffle or thimble of sweet raisins are given free of charge with your coffee, and how a certain amount of human filth is included in the accounting of its organization.

Twice a week, the interns – two students from Cooper Union – came in to do time at the office. Keiko and Scott were the bane of Maris's existence. The idea to hire interns was a cost-cutting impulse, but Maris now spent twice as much time explaining what was to be done as it would have taken to do it herself. These kids put her in a state of panic because there really was not much to do, and there's nothing more aggravating than having to explain nothing to two eager-beaver interns. On the other hand, Maris lost her temper when they brought in their school work. She hated the energy of people reading around her desk. Sometimes Maris had them clean Codax's brushes. Today she gives in and lets them edit a press release before sending it out. She tells them to only add to it, one phrase to each sentence. And don't make so much noise with the keyboard. Meanwhile, Maris pretends to work at her computer, typing a mile a minute, adding chapter after chapter to her automatic memoir.

FOR IMMEDIATE RELEASE: I loved talking to you last night, even as I was squirming in my own discomfort of being. I live in a cruel little room, and I'm getting to know it intimately. Forget about masturbating, these days I'm into crying. Sometimes I spend hours lying on my bathroom floor, looking up at the sky through a little skylight. This is not discouraging at all, it is damned inspiring.

The tense hour is long gone and time keeps burning like a jet engine. Everything here proceeds with an almost erotic sensitivity to time's never-ending suicide. Everything and everybody goes into it. Maris laughs for the first time all day: Reena has put another tack on her chair. Reena laughs too and takes another swig off Codax's Remy. Pestered enough, Codax finally agrees to paint her portrait. A glossy black spill. It takes him five seconds to do. Soon those pretentious C.R.A.K. boys will be here. Maris needs them to sign something. Reena busies herself constructing a wobbly barricade around Codax with office chairs.

Maris is seeing it now. She is back in the saddle. Shape and defy this world. She smells the big show. The lived moment. The population of the office has almost tripled. A casting call in progress. Maris is updating herself and the city again. Reena loves it when she does this. They do it together.

Reena speaker-phones Keiko to go over and ask Codax if he will paint the sets for *Cinema of The Damned*, or *Battle On Broadway* – she is still torn between these two titles, so she will use both. Maris has some very good news about the budget. Jef Martinet is in the elevator. Reena finishes her soup, puts her feet up on the desk, and belches as loud as she can. She watches Maris's migraine come on as she practices her opening number, using her elbows and thighs as resonators and singing Maris all the way to the medicine cabinet. She practices spitting at the audience.

FOR IMMEDIATE RELEASE: Maris Parings desires your presence at *Cinema of The Damned*, a live spectacle featuring Reena Spaulings and C.R.A.K. 10pm sharp. Free beer. All ages welcome. Death to the pigs!

Chapter 18

Manhattan On Your Hands and Knees

The 'deck hands' paused and looked up at the sounds of commotion from the gangplank. Maris, too, paused in the knot she was tying, drawing the cheroot from her mouth and squinting against the 'morning sun.' The 'coast' was a bright green, looming behind the brilliant chaos of the port, and the 'air' was thick with the suggestion of cargo and the decay and death that permeated this ragged shore. She cast down the cheroot, grinding it into the worn deck with her heel as she stepped to the railing. Several white men – dressed as Englishmen – were surrounded by Arabian porters, apparently held up as they were attempting to board.

"You've no right!" cried the 'English' leader indignantly, pulling the folds of an absurdly dandyish coat around him. A towering 'Nubian' blocking the way stood impassively, the gold hoops in his ears catching the light and shivering it into a thousand cold slivers.

"You!" Maris said, making a slight gesture with her hand. At her voice, the group turned their heads as one, seeming to detect in those tones something powerful, and perhaps a bit mad. The leader of the troupe immediately launched into a speech, apparently grasping at the new hope of a white woman who might take their side. His face was pasty and soft, and yet he, like all four of them, was streaked with dirt, and looked as if he hadn't eaten in a while.

"You must tell this Negro to stand down," he said petulantly. "We're in a hurry to leave this accursed place – surely you understand, someone as commanding as you..." he stopped himself suddenly, as if sensing that this might not be the right backside to kiss.

"Where do you hail from?" Maris said.

"From Pennsylvania," he said uncertainly.

Maris laid a hand on the shoulder of the 'Nubian', who silently melted aside to let the group pass. They straggled up the plank, casting insolent looks at the surly-faced onlookers. Behind them, the sounds of men working resumed, as the incident was laid aside and the morning's trade continued.

Then stepping into the heat of a hundred lamps, Reena busts out with three tiger leaps in quick succession and, slipping in a pool of spilled beer, comes down hard on her skull. The music, clarinets, come down like a wave and the theater is gone.

That's when they all had to improvise as if their lives depended on it. Especially the police, who arrived with their own nets, new orange ones made of bendy plastic that could immobilize a dozen agitators at a time. And they didn't like that, to be stopped in a net in the middle of their opening number. They kept singing. Singing and swinging.

A-Rod began to swing his bat. They took him down like a dog, with an acoustical weapon, and the people couldn't stand to see it. The people? Well now they imagined themselves exactly like that, as the people. There was the people hallucination, suddenly.

It wasn't like here, now. There were a lot of differences. For example, the music. There were clarinets and helicopters, plus the acoustical weapons, like you never heard. And the storming of the stage, the dressing room incident, and all the suddenly empty seats. All at once, like choreography. In Argentina, in 2000, people swarmed the meat trucks and hallucinated and took everything.

Causing panic. Causing erections. My first thought, like day one. It gets into you, another music in the eyes and nerves. Thinks you. Coming up out of the subway, a lovely big pussy smile on your face.

She lost control again in Times Square. She ran toward the river. She, meaning everybody involved, meaning the riot. Go ahead, Zou…

I'm Chanqyn Zou, 32, of Chinatown. See my chest and arm? No comment. Okay slow language. I tell you what. Big problems with cops. Noisy, noisy, lotta noise outside. Zou at Red Rose hotspot, in basement, in one asian hotspot, okay? Here noise. Go out. Why? Why noise, police? So many! Everywhere. Party? No party! Party? Incident. Numerous gun bullets, blood, spots of blood. I see like slow, go slow legs, everything fast fast. I see Reena. I tell you, now, a lady. Bullet chest. No, lady! I help. I say, "bouncer, Red Rose bouncer, Red Rose waitress, help." I hate police, New York police. I am Chinese language problem, but I say now: I hate. My feeling like that. This lady Reena like she's a queen lady, a rose! First Class. I see, I know, I know. Zou, bouncer get her in, Reena in hotspot now, okay? Her chest, o. No comment. I take care. I'm nice guy, not all the time…human. Police plobe, try identify. What for? They say numerous violation. So! Everywhere! Now, many fight, fight in theater, fight in river, all over fight. Swim and fighting, so many fighting. What? River fight? Okay, why not something I don't know. Once in your life. And gunshot, gunshot, shit. One, two die, two, two. I see that! My too eyes. Smoke. Long time fight. Why? I go out, too much. I go down. Reena leave. Where to? No idea. Okay? You tell me.

If a burlesque actor's body is the primary material of its film's action, Reena too can be thought of as a material. Like the spectacle she's starring in, Reena is repeatedly destroyed and reanimated: she is put to work, drugged, made into an advertising image, fucked, robbed, paid, made to speak, shut up, desired by individuals and abandoned in crowds, erased, rewritten and rehashed. And like a burlesque actor, Reena endlessly survives her treatment. In this chapter, Reena is at the center of a disaster, a musical riot in Manhattan. She has also been shot, but it is only a surface wound.

A quick-thinking Mr. Zou improvises a bandage for her with cocktail napkins and tape, and then she is on her feet again and takes off. All around us the city is surging, and as sometimes happens in a musical riot, we suddenly find ourselves alone.

"The building is closed, Miss."

The revolving door she goes through every day to get to the office. It is not revolving. On the other side of the glass, the guard's shadowy figure approaches. Then, a flashlight beam in her eyes.

"Closed!"

The door is not revolving. The guard is frozen in the glass, not too close, behind his beam.

"Miss, I can't let you in. Building policy."

She can see the little lights on the elevators, down a long dim stretch of marble. The colossal Frank Stella asleep on the wall. Superimposed on all this, a festival of police lights in the glass.

"Sorry."

The guard goes back to his station, taking his sweet time, and sits. He buries himself in his sports section, in the distance.

At this moment Reena is off the radar, but that's okay. There are these moments of dead time, when you've lost your character, lost the tune, and you just wander. These too are moments of improvisation, times when if you came to see me I would draw you for free. I'm a Chinese portrait artist writing back at you. You're not a P.A. I am.

We can say with some certainty that Reena stops in a bar. She wants a drink. Wild Turkey, no ice. A double.

We can say with some certainty that Reena stops in a bar. She wants a drink. Wild Turkey, no ice. A double. She's in McHale's Bar on 46th and 8th in a back room watching TV (SNL). (Must be a re-run). I'm there with my report card checking my college grades. I'm looking for my GPA – at the quarter. I have an "A" in Riflery, a "B" in theater (always got a B) and a "10" in some General Studies class I'm struggling with.

But I wind up talking to Reena who is alone and doesn't remember that we hooked up before.

We get flirty and she's acting very strange, like celebrities do. I don't hide the fact that I know her – but I say I've seen her on TV instead. And I draw attention to my attempts to be funny. "Don't you hate when people try to be funny?" "That was a lame joke."

But I'm still cracking myself up (maybe nerves)

I'm happy to mess around with her and happy to pretend we never met.

There is a bed.

…a fold-out bed in the back of the bar. We are fooling around – I make her come – and afterwards she says, "What would you like me to do to you?" (a blow-job?) I seem to remember sex was out of the question from the last time. We're kissing which is nice. But I say, "I just want to hold you" and I mean it. I just want to feel her body close to mine.

I feel she's a little unnerved by this. I decide I'm not going to push for anything. Just relax and be polite, and be direct. Afterward, she says, "Oops, here comes my boyfriend." And I believe she may be telling the truth. I make a joke and start looking for weapon (not joking) – find a metal door jamb that's bendy – good for whipping. But she's bluffing- trying to see how I react. She's odd – asks me what I'm doing now – I have to go see this band – you're welcome to come (I actually have 2 bands that I need to see @ 12:00 and 12:30, and I'm already late for the 12 – it's part of my report card).

This surprises her, too – I feel.

Perhaps she's used to being the one with somewhere to go. I feel her interest in me rise – I enjoy being the coy one – we're playing these games as we get dressed. In the back of a bar in mid-town. It seems like they know her here. She acts at home.

(pause)

And now I'M at McHale's. In the bathroom the sailor takes a crap looking at me. He asks me how I'm doing. How much is that

hat? How much are those shoes? I'll pay a lot but not for pussy. They steal your monay. And there's no recourse. Excuse me, can I ask you a question? (No, thanks.) Okay. Faggot. Little faggot motherfucker. I'll walk with you...I'll walk when you walk...I'll smile when you smile...I'll fight when you fight...I'll be nice when you be nice...This is MY neighborhood. How long have you lived in this neighborhood?...(5 years) ... 5 years? (Yeah.) I've lived here for 50 years. (Why are you a sailor?) What are you? (I'm a P.A.) What do think would happen if you and me went round the corner and fight right now. Huh? I'm betting on me. Who you gonna bet? Your girl is a cunt. (She's not my girl) I don't give a fuck what she is, she's a cunt...(I'm not afraid of you) I never said you're afraid of me! ...I'm a generous person. If I see a child drowning I jump in...You keep walking ...You're a punk motherfucker. AND YOUR DADDY IS ASHAMED TO CALL YOU HIS SON.

Exist on the second level of Times Square, for example, 42nd Street. But on the second level. It's better...

Don't pantomime this.

The colors. The colors bold brush stroke. Slap it on. Like this. Nyuk...In front of MoMA earlier (I'm a Asian dude with dark skin and dreads. I get high a lot Rich.) MoMA for lunch. Times Square for dinner. People walking in the street. The flow. The public goes. My easel. Get the floes. The light likes my walk...You're too close to me. Move a little bit. (Protecting my mystique.) Walking west.

"Real live coed girls working their way thru college."

Chambers Street was good because I speak Chinese. (But I speak Chinese cos I don't speak English!)

Now at Madame Tussaud's... a man jumped to his death after the voices from the crowd said "Jump!" "Do it!!" And he did. "Cool. I wanna see a dead body!" and "I don't wanna see a dead body."

(Remember the marquees had haikus on them? That was cool.)

The black duvateen masks the performers and the sex on the

second floor but still audition. Those with licenses get in the van (everyone) Selling/Painting portraits at the Art Expo near Jacob Javits. Fights break out with Security. Jim is thrown in the wagon. John Kelsey isn't there, but if he was, he would not be in the wagon. …Cops descend. Too close for comfort. No, sit close to me. Sit here. What do you like to do? "I'm not a Portrait Artist. Don't claim that I am." I'm have to run away from this.

On the street…Walking west on 42nd street. <u>WAY WEST</u>. Walking. walking. If I hang on (let it hang). If we kiss it won't mean anything. If I can hang on to Touch the water touches water the shoe water fight fighting the water wagon fighting fighting fighting more fighting fighting fighting swimming fighting fighting they're fighting (keep in mind, <u>I don't know English</u>) fighting in Hudson River fighting fighting swimming FIGHTING FIGHTING SWIMMING FIGHTING FIGHTING SWIMMING SWIMMING SWIMMING FIGHTING SWIMMING FIGHTING FIGHTING

FIGHTING

(sings)

I AM A P.A.
YOU ARE NOT
A P.A.

RUB IT OUT

I AM A P.A.
YOU ARE NOT
A P

A

<u>KISS ME</u>
I'M A P.A.

<u>KISS ME</u>
I'm a p.a

<u>KISS ME</u>

<u>KISS MY MOUTH</u>

I'M <u>THE</u> P.A.

Hello, hello. Mums for sale half price, eucalyptus trees, buckets full of mandarines, wads of carrots, packs of cigarettes. There is a fantastic smell in the air. Finally it's Saturday. My favorite day of the week, since childhood. There was always the smell of something fresh in it. Like grass, or fires in the garden, potato-eater-stuff (poverty in the early '60s in Germany). Saturday always carried thoughts and scents of freedom. 333 small bells are ringing, all so alive. Saturday forever.

Already, a new kind of world is in front of us. Nobody saw it coming, nobody at all, nie me nor thee. We didn't see it.

Come in, or go out, but do go now.

Burger King on Canal Street, R&B BGM, a place for a date. Cartoon traffic dividers near Madison Park, 23rd & 5th, night. Hotel Whirlpools on 24th bet 5th & 6th – to investigate. Leonia, NJ, an apartment building called The Marlborough House, on Grand Ave above Highway 93. Cavernous streets in the financial district: 80 Pine St., near Pearl, going up towards Chase building; up Pine from Water St; up Hanover St. and Beaver; down Gold St. and John. In Italy in the Apines under the Gran Sasso, there is a lab and a telescope. 5:03 pm, late October; on the East river promenade at 79th St. The setting sun lights up the primitive apartment blocks of Roosevelt Island. On the other side of the walk is the rushing traffic of Roosevelt Drive. A sailboat sails past for an idyllic contrast. As the Reena character continues to walk, a police boat rushes past too, close to the shore, its wake stirring up waves against the concrete.

What are you doing tonight?

Reena is a ruin. She climbs the steps to her apartment, which she hasn't stepped foot into in days, collapses in her fancy office chair, setting the vibrating massage function to low, and immediately falls asleep.

The words have a particular way of sitting just on top of the paper. The rounded back of the s, the heavy ass of the d. Slow down, Spaulings, stop. Dump some dimes'n dat slot dare. Slow dance. Sexy song. Sip drink. Sit, slouch. Say, "Damn." Suck dick. Snake dong. Sleep, dream, something different.

Chapter 19

O ne time we went down by the freight tracks, found a black tire and we burned it to a smoldering mess, and got in trouble afterwards with the train yards... Like, what were you all thinking, what the HELL were you thinking, oh, well, you know we didn't mean anything serious, sorry, we didn't know it couldn't be put out...

The dark screens of the TV monitors seemed to accompany me constantly as I moved about the room. They followed me. There was one in the bed and one on a chair. When I stood still, I could just about see both screens at once. The one in bed was sturdy, probably quite chunky and heavy. The screen on the chair was plasma and smooth. It did not seem to be set or attached. It had a light plastic base so it could be swiveled up and down and left to right. The bed screen was squat and square. The chair screen had some kind of new technology and was getting my attention. Although the room was comfortable and luxurious, I was a bit nervous and distracted in there. In order to prevent my heart from racing uncomfortably, I had to concentrate and keep calm. Both screens flickered on to blue and filled me with an oppressive sense of hope. I only took maintenance drugs once in my life. It was a period of extreme anxiety.

One evening, after a relaxing bath and a nice meal, I watched a video clip countdown from 1000 to 1. A moderator appeared between each music video to present interesting facts around what was being shown, to keep the flow going as harmlessly and carelessly as tap water. A pop singer wearing a black turtleneck played guitar for the camera. Her black eyelashes batted up and down, slicing her grey green eyes open. Her black black pupils darted shyly and with deep reproach. This is very, very exciting. I wanted to call somebody, a friend, to let them know what was happening. My mind was racing. I had to walk around a little. In doing so, I passed the other screen on the chair and impulsively switched that on too. A famous artist appeared immediately, introducing his newest art works. These were huge towers balanced on enormous lead books that would fall down one day but he did not care, he said. Now both screens were on. I could watch them at the same time. I wanted to go out and see people and talk about everything I saw.

Later on, once it was dark outside, and the wind was blowing gustily around the city rooftops, and there was nothing but the night approaching, I again broke into the silence of the screens. They had porn films for me. One was about someone who was very unhappy and wanted to have sex and love at the same time, whereas friends and acquaintances were getting lots of sex everywhere and seemed very happy. The other was about a boy who masturbated in the attic quite a lot. There was also a girl in a neighboring building who lifted up her skirt. All stars fell in a bowl of mud that night. I responded with receptiveness and openness, and began to smile. In a mood of gentle sadness, I turned myself off.

What is it?

The very thick crust of a pot of violets in a Fautrier painting. A little black spill. A deluge. Pot black, shoe black, bower black, all bleeding together. Skullfuckingly heavy nature alternating with moments that almost turn blue. De-spectacle-ized monsters come out of the sea. You fall on your face, you fall in the mud. Nobody is picking you up. You make a mud sculpture. Mud on mud. Dust. Her spectacles fell off into a complex sea of darkness. Enter the lengthy labyrinth of dust and divine filth. A never-ending obsession, with interpreting context extracted from a cloud. Alchemical dislocation giving way to masochistic disorientation. Everything so goddamn wrong yet so skullfingeringly right. Skronk-intensive beats till darkness turns see-thru. Celebrated communications breakdowns. A kick of a boot, a thought shot into the night, sunglasses at all times. Exploded blackout in a cave. Held-in-suspense forever. Pure potentiality. Utmost extremity. Shooting into the dark with two massive strobes on, catching nothing in their beams. To enter: cerebral emptiness, the suspension of the suspension. The nothingness has become a bit rougher lately; nevertheless it is emotive as hell. Should we give free passage to visions, saddle up the nightmares and gallop away? All manic directions speed towards the abyss. Betrayals at parties, smokes, empty worlds, new black ensembles, black sunrise, and win win win in the black zone. The gamble, bling bling l'amour, glamour, the apocalyptic rise, the timeless black desire, of which the underground scene reports: "Into the shit we go!" The highest order of glossy thin evil has grown and bloomed wildly, lately, where catharsis is put on thick like the worst makeup job ever seen. We all hate her shoes. Salutti per tutti! Most abstract day by day, night by night re-enter the magic and music of despair and lust. Flames of night are flickering high. We spit and celebrate. Show your theatre now, show your darkness. The gothic carnival is on. Black chemical hair. Shaved eyebrows. Burnt toast. Karl Lagerfeld's reductive black method. And the white is only there to enter the blackness. Cinema of the Damned. Torture films in 16mm, scratched celluloid and ripped sprocket holes. An army of projectors, streaming video flows, row upon row of headless spectators.

"Sitting on a hillside, watching all the people die. They'll feel much better on the other side." Feast of screams and laughter. Painting minds with clouds of blackface. Dancing in the enormous swamp where strange black flares spill and stink, a conga line swells and suicides. Stuck in the swamp, waiting for more zombies to emerge from the black slime. I told you, cross the space limit! Where was the Black Cabaret where we met? You were a hovering ghost, just out of the moment. Nothing ever ends until you let it go. There are emerging black lines, unruly, talking, symbolic left-overs. A shop window on St. Mark's Place holds the death of a civilization, oh my little black scraps. Pour over all this broken liquid glass. A process-demonstration. A crusty, splintering, ugly surface. Open wound, not healed but just frozen in mid-spill. Unreproducible. Hey, Black Metal, Black Metal, Black Metal. Void dwellers. Nihilistic spelunkers. Little dark thrones. Immortality! Take it it's yours! The Bitch Witch with long voluptuous oscillation and crazy bangs from the dark sorority, and her laughter of exploding stars. She is polished like a shoe on a holiday, ready to step into the bigshit, urban dungeons, subway tunnels, pitchblack propaganda, fuckedupandreadytodie. Stuck in a solo mode, weaving through massive fascisms. Only you enter temples, obsessive loves, desires, your night bedomiongdoing an unclassifiable encreaterur. Fly into a doomed concert. A music of existential resonance, moving toward a megalith that collapses into a self-negating nothing, into you. "Only the impossible is worth the effort." Materialist music rendered with unconditional love, black noise, a crashing temporarily suspending all rules of sound. Now there is screaming feedbacks and sonic bliss, there is a mashing of ideas and sounds, sonic denseness, free screech, extreme attack, and raw dirt. Slayer of nowhere, electrophilia, daughter of x? Even after the show, the hum and buzz continues in your head. A hundred goblins came to town and snuck around, and they are still looking for you.

A black cat disappears into a dark hole and loses its way. Deeper and deeper, she wanders for all eternity in the land of beetles and snakes, its meows fading out, fading out. A black widow spider is waiting in the dark. The spider stings her and she dies.

A raven in a velvet cage. Feeding him a piece of licorice. Feeding him blackberries. Reflected in his bottomless, black eyes: Total silence.

How long has she been gone? She called out. A muffled, dull cry coming from the inside of a box or the trunk of a car. Her head weighed a hundred pounds. Then fuzz.

Reena walks cautiously ahead; there's another turn in the passage. Something pinkish and red flashes across her eyelids, so fast that it takes her a moment to realize it's just a colorful mental residue in her head and not a light in the distance. The floor feels smooth but with small grooves in it, a grid, a giant bathroom tile floor in white, and she can feel the white against her stomach because now she is crawling. Her knuckles tap on someone's foot.

"They call me Shade. I have stood here for many ages."

The figure called Shade helps Reena to her feet and slaps her silly.

An oil tanker capsizes in the Black Sea in the dead of night. An oil slick spreading over a nocturnal bed of mussels. I know this is the end. I can either wait and drown slowly in this thick liquid, or make a noose with your fishnets and hang myself from the charred beams above.

"The building is closed, Miss."

A black square. Expensive underwear. A window sealed with gaffer's tape and thick duvateen. Amplifiers. A limousine parked in the dark. A blind butler kneeling down to tie my patent leather shoe. A black-out, anarchy.

"Miss, I can't let you in. Building policy."

My top hat has blown off my head and landed in a tar pit. Reaching into the darkness with my ebony cane, trying to fish it out. It sinks slowly. I can't see anything.

"Sorry."

Shade nods and wavers, coughs up a gob of phlegm and spits into Reena's face.

Groping and sometimes bumping heads with other pedestrians in the dark. Traveling on foot. Distances open up, the blacked-out New York skyline. Trying to make out the shape of the Empire State building against the night sky.

Shade offers Reena a black plate with three thick lines of brown heroin that are glazed over and unreachable.

"Love is the color night meets at night. Black is the color of Bruges and black is the color of white night, black black needs, long hair, freshers ball, black black Huddersfield man. Black as the black of thought, black is the black of Monday night."

Leaving Shade behind and inching along on her belly, Reena listened. Another straight section ahead, that's what her ears told her with the echo of some sound that would rise up in a barely audible whisper. Awakening on her back, surprised to find herself having slept while leaning against a wall, there was the steady drumming of water rushing beneath her. Perhaps she was several levels above the huge waterfall where all the sewers meet. Involuntarily she jumped as a nerve spasm electrified her lower body for a second.

On nights like this, the hours until the morning are the longest. For a child, it might be the hours of waiting before an exciting voyage, Christmas, a birthday, or the arrival of a much-loved relative. Reena remembered these as the most mysterious nights of her life, before gradually they dropped off to be replaced by nights of involuntary thinking, drugs, alcohol and anxiety. She tried to concentrate on counting the layers of blackness between the ceiling and her body. She tried to let the warmth of her body pull her away from consciousness. She tried and failed, tried and failed, hoping that even this pathetic rhythm would tire her out. Letting her mind wander and turning prophetic, Reena anticipated the day when she would leave everything behind and betray all her new friends. She imagined someplace out in the cold, across snowy fields, where something special was waiting for her. A solitary little tree with a bottle of ink hanging from it, slowly dripping drops of black ink on the snow. A present without a name on it, a secret hinting at new and more dangerous loyalties.

Inky.

A prayer for Maris, who dies a violent death every night in my dreams. God save her from this fate. A prayer for Lizzi, Bernadette, Giorgio, and all the others who, by doing nothing, provided me with energy holes to float in and eyes so that I could show up. May their recipes win top prizes some day. A prayer for Michael, the last true dandy on earth, and may he be remembered as the supremely generous soul he never could admit he was. Michael, your paintings really suck and I'm glad you know it. A prayer for the Shlappy boys. They always provided the perfect human décor and never let the party get too ugly. And a prayer for Garson, who didn't deserve to drown but looked so good as he went under. May god forgive me for the pleasure I took in seeing him plunge over the rails, a pleasure that never seems to fade. I'm glad he made it.

The big nothing was coming down the street, churning up slow motion dust clouds as it approached. Every contour was etched and vivid. Solid, fluid motion, carrying forward with a pitiless momentum. It was bathed in some chemical infusion that seemed to make it absorb light. It could crush you under gallons of slow motion muddy water. The closer it came, the smaller everything got.

The big nothing beheaded Reena every hour on the hour. Beheaded again, she began to play with herself, mentally Krebbering pictures of Maris in the shower. But she couldn't bring herself off, and was beheaded again after twenty minutes imagining her boss's dark, brazilianed, stressed out cunt pressed up against her face. Beheaded and bored, Reena rolled over.

An old man was looking in the window. Could he see Reena? He had his gray, beheaded face pressed up to the glass with that Sunday afternoon "just looking" or "just beheaded" look that old people tend to have when they kill time window gazing while waiting for their prescriptions to be filled. It was a beheaded look. He was like a moth, helplessly drawn to the window but as if not really seeing anything, neither himself nor what was on the other side of the glass. Drawn there and fixed in an attraction. Reena sat very still in her towel, not at all sure if she was being seen but definitely seeing. Did he know that she was seeing him? Maybe there was too much glare on his side of the glass. It was a long, strange moment during which Reena was torn between two feelings: being pinned down by what she felt in every part of her as the old man's beheaded stare; but also embarrassment at the indiscretion of her own gaze and the helplessness of the quite possibly blinded voyeur outside her window. The man stood there for ten minutes at least, giving Reena all the time in the world to contemplate his lost, old moth face. She wanted to cry. Crying now, she let her towel slip a little, and the man backed off. Then another man appeared, even more gray and beheaded. And a hunch-backed old lady wheeled herself into view. They stood and stared, maybe waiting for Reena to reveal herself, maybe not even seeing her.

Meanwhile, a trail of ants moved between a crack in the wall and a half-eaten bowl on the floor by the TV. The black trail moved in two directions at once, to and from their invisible nest. A closed circuit, incapable of distraction. Do ants get bored of being ants? This ability to behead oneself with ants or plants.

I went out into the woods to make my snares and deadfalls. I didn't do it for the furs: I could get all the pelt I wanted driving up and down the Merritt Parkway scraping carcasses. No. I wanted to prove to myself I could do it the old way, and to work my way up the ladder: rabbit snare, otter deadfall, coon deadfall, marten deadfall, bear deadfall, bear pen. Yes. But what the hell would I do with a live bear in a pen? I'd cross that bridge when I got there. I decided to go out at night to actually see the animals entering and being crushed in the deadfalls. I went out every night in the cold, waiting in the dark at each deadfall, but never saw a damn thing. It became a letdown even seeing the deadfalls with animals in them. I wanted to see them die, or nothing. But I had reserved some thrill for any bear, live or dead, which I had never managed to catch. It was two years after I started this enterprise that, creeping up to a bear deadfall I had erected months before in early winter (now it was almost spring), I noticed it had collapsed. I waited a long time looking at it there from a distance, expecting the bear to hurl aside the paltry tinder and come surging out at me. There was no surging. I strode in a little angry, seeing no apparent bulk heaping up the timbers, so I started casting them aside, figuring it had collapsed on its own. This sometimes happens. How long had my deadfall been in this useless state? Then one log lifted revealed a small black arm. Human. A kid playing in the woods.

During the days that followed, Reena walked the corridors and grounds of Bissenmoor Estate, her eyes focused on nothing. She rarely heard anyone say a word to her and didn't know whether she was able to speak or not. One afternoon while it rained, she sat on a bench in the garden and then she discovered that she was completely dry. Or should it be said that she began to see everything clearly for the first time? The stain of immoral resignation, encouraged by a soft voice, had ruined any chances of finding something to do with herself.

If I give up my life in order to live and be ruined, I am satisfied and wounded, torn apart. Anything divine is executed on the surface. Over my head is an ecstatic outpouring always ready to take place. Intimacy can break down any two people in the right places. I have emotions in these situations. That is why I laugh more often than I think.

Reena let him take the blanket out from under her arm and watched him spread it over a patch of grass. He emptied the satchel and beckoned to her. She looked around and hesitated, so he reached up to take her arm and pull it towards the small black grenades. She forgot where she was for the moment. The little bombs were amazing. They looked like black sticks of deodorant. He moved his hands smoothly over the devices, demonstrating how to arm and detonate them. Her chest felt tight. Soon the rush of her blood curved the gloom in her heart, until she felt passionately involved. She opened myself eagerly and the result was obvious. The foulest proposal had managed to crush a hunger she was only ever slightly aware of. By the time they were finished, tears were streaming down Reena's face.

The water battered her face faster and harder as she continued walking through the darkness. Cars and trucks rushed by, some honking their horns, but she walked on and on until she came to a gas station. It was closed, but there was a telephone booth next to it. She dialed the number on the slip of paper in her pocket.

If I do this, will we have a chance together? A warm body in the night, I say it warms my soul. I long for interstellar degradation. Passions for nothing, a conspiracy heading nowhere human at all.

At the first chord, Smith and Carlos bowed their heads and raised their clenched fists to the sky. On each was a black glove. Norman didn't raise his fist, but he too was making a protest. The crowd's initial reaction to the actions of the athletes was stunned silence. Then, as they realized what they were witnessing, many in the large American contingent started to whistle and boo; others sang the American national anthem as loud as they could. The medallists stood there and endured it. Neither Smith nor Carlos wore shoes, just black socks. Smith wore a black scarf, Carlos black beads – in remembrance of lynchings. Smith would later explain that his raised right hand stood for the power in black America, Carlos's raised left hand, for the unity of black America. The black scarf round his neck stood for black pride. The black socks with no shoes stood for black poverty in racist America. The totality of our effort is the regaining of black dignity.

She wakes up, has no idea where she is. Where am I? The bed moves. Something is getting into bed with her, another person breathing next to her. "Hi." Another body, cold, naked, pressing up against hers. She recoils and strains to see who it is, but all she sees is darkness and an armpit. Darkness and an armpit deep enough to reach back and pull over her own shadowy heart.

Black, black, and blacker still. A tremendous expansion ensues, overflowing backwards, filling up the ruts and trenches long left behind, not really forgotten and yet abandoned. It shall run as long and wide as it has to, this famous flow that lays down the rules that work cannot keep up with. It is completely absent-minded, not even mindful of the fear that keeps the present as an over-lived result, the history of my calamity.

She sighed deeply and gave up waiting. The dark clouds that had covered the moon slipped off and the pale white light illuminated the road, making it look like a trail of bones that led still to a happy life, that is, a trail of bones leading somewhere certain, like a town or city. She made a decision back there, she thought. There was nothing to do now but carry it out. She started to walk again.

It was a tall young man who had remained standing perfectly still in a doorway two houses down. He stepped out into the street and walking up rapidly flung another bomb over the heads of the crowd. It actually struck the Director on the shoulder as he stooped over his dying friend, then falling between his feet exploded with a terrific concentrated boom, striking him dead to the ground, finishing the wounded man and practically annihilating the empty car. With a yell of horror the crowd broke up and fled in all directions, except for those who fell dead or dying where they stood nearest to the director, and one or two others who did not fall till they had run a little.

The very thick crust of a pot of violets in a Fautrier painting. The layer under the skin of a naked girl painted by Balthus. An overcrowded street at night in Berlin in the '20s painted by George Grosz. The color of ink. It arrives with no announcement.

Bridges are falling down. The news propels my breath, switching it from left to right. My knees now want to walk, so I go out further, to the nearest bridge, the one next door, an old bridge, with an older river flowing beneath it. Crossing it, I wait for it to fall, reach the other side, and then cross again with heavier footsteps this time, to let it know what progress means. Twice across is enough, my work is done. Now back home to rest, prepare for sleep. It is 4 o'clock, ten hours to go. Enough time to reassemble the same women and men around the same dark circle, another repetition of the interplay of energies which now storm this planet – the greatest glory hole in the universe.

Stepping out into the heat of a hundred lamps, Reena busts three tiger leaps in quick succession and, slipping in a pool of spilled beer, comes down hard on her skull. The music, clarinets, come down on her like a wave and the theater is gone. Forever. For now, a black chapter in our days.

Chapter 20

GREAT MEETING YOU

W ell, today is Thanksgiving and you know you can't find a
real turkey anywhere around these alps unless you go to the
market and pick it and kill it yourself. Yes, really you can do that,
but instead we had group FONDUE: everyone sat around the
table and took bread crumbs, drank white wine and dipped it in the
hot melted cheese. Everyone was German and speaking mostly
German. I brought my good American man Roger and we talked
english...louder! *Natürlich!*

Last week was the local town country fair with cows and pigs
and horses, cheap rides, tons of local vino, wonderful deer and
horse meats, and cheeses galore. Did I tell you how yummy deer
and horse is? Anyway, there was a cow fashion show and it was
amazing, and the biggest pumpkin in all of Switzerland was there.
In the wine tent hosted by a bank, a fight broke out. The guy was
so drunk. He stood up fast, the table fell on top of him and he
jumped on a kid and threw the kid at the other guy. It was horrible
and amazing. And picture it: there was the sound of the accordion
and 3 men and one busted woman, I think a woman, with a
Morganna not-ashed cig singing sad Italian songs and didn't stop.
I met a cute big Italian young bear who was all over me, then he
actually scared me...when usually I scare others...and well he was
17...shows you I'm turning over that leaf...the day was bound to
happen.

Tomorrow I'm flying to London to visit my mom and hang out with her and get some city life back in me. I have become so slow and I'm so nervous to go back to a big city after all that....

You really scared the fuck out of me. You always did. In your streets I felt the irresistible pressure of having plenty of space to suffocate in. You were like one big zoological park and every monkey had its designated plot for atrophy. Yours was the most brutal example of freedom I'd ever experienced. Nothing could happen in you.

But you were so wonderful in so many ways. The accumulation of insanity and hopes. You, the Will To Power-bar I enjoyed sucking on. No taste at all! Ghastly in the light, exciting and mysterious in the dark. The stimulant supreme. The garbage, the sidewalks. All the people to strangle. All the people to have sex with. A Billion potential encounters. You possessed the ultimate allure of illusions. Enter to win, enter to lose, enter to not-be, somewhere in-between the grid, the metro musics, the parties. We said fuck you, Berlin, London, because in New York we were sweating the evil they would be photocopying in three years' time.

Though I went to Milano last week and it was hot. I went to this great bar in the middle of dirty whore città called COMPANY. It was great. I think it was a convention of the short bears society. They were all under 5ft and some were muscles and some were bloody ugly boars. But to each their own. I met this guy named Alfredo...and well he was my dream. 6ft. Tanned, black goatee, light italian blue eyes, big hands, hairy chest you could see through his worn out United States Navy white t-shirt. And a sailor hat to top it off. Got a nice present (besides a phone number snuck in my hand): I got his finger up my hole. That was an interesting treat. And yes I am a European virgin, practically. Okay I have done it once, but that was the first month. Arrgh. So difficult living up on an alp.

I have to say this past week was rough starting at yes 8 am, even 7:30 am today, and it has also been a bit emotional. I was watching

SEX in the CITY in German. Yes they have it perfectly dubbed over and they don't know the ending of the show here, though in Italy I heard they do. We only have German TV. I have tried to get some Italian stations but these Germans don't budge and they have pre-programmed it that way. That's fine. I mean German POP STARS are hilarious and so much more exciting, maybe because they are worse or maybe cuz they are more mean. After a bottle of vino rossi it's the best thing and the only thing in the world. Well anyway. I was saying I was drinking my wine and it was the episode when Carrie realizes everything is changing in NYC. When the lady asks her for SITuations in the bathroom and she falls out the window. And I got so homesick for the first time. Then I read that article JOHN G sent me from NEW YORK magazine saying how it's the end of the hipsters pretty much and that everyone is leaving NYC. It's dead. I don't really miss the city.

You see? Your love is circular. There's nothing like it. It makes us forget how to change. Your senseless complexity, your glorious gentrification nightmares. I love how you always make us go back to the starting points. We keep losing everything. Suffering from your love, we love your love. Loving you is throwing stuff blindly. But this is only a small little something to say, a breath of writing that takes place in the suspension of time between two moments, expressing and not expressing my love and devotion to you. Yes, I wanted to tell you that the most ridiculously pathetic scenes are to be taken seriously.

Reality is not capitalist, get that through your head! I'll never get my blood back that I mixed into your bucket. I'll never pull my thing out of your thing. When I see you be so ridiculous to some-one I love, and deal your stupid jealous death-blows I hate you. Pull the plug, I don't care, I'm tired of you. You once told me: by putting the experience of emotional intensities in common, you go against what living beings desire most, namely peace and quiet. I guess this is war. What a year. On the other hand, I have nothing against the peace and quiet that any living being, as a living being, carries within him. "Life is sweet": any blade of grass knows this better than all the citizens of the world. I miss you very much. Some of you got drunk-n-dial calls. Thank you for being there. It's been over 3 months now since all that whatever and well I thought I would just say it: hasn't time flown by.

I'm trying to wangle my way out of my obligations because I need long hours to do nothing, which I consider to be a big part of my work now. Don't be alarmed too much I guess, and don't take this note to be a real letter. It was written when the shit was probably hitting the fan. I'm so tired I'm spilling around like water, and seeing crazy-bugs on the floor and on the stove. Wow. I guess I'm dead! It's intense. As far as money goes, this summer totally ruined me for the winter but so what. Time flies when one is obsessed and I am.

Well, farewell my friend. For my part, I'm returning to my *mania*, which I can be induced to abandon only by something as great as the joy or grief of one of my friends, and I'm disappearing for a long time. When I see you again, it will be something truly beautiful and glorious.

About the author

Bernadette Corporation was founded in a nightclub in 1994. Hired to attract attractive young people to parties and events, Bernadette Corporation soon became more interested in organizing spontaneous, purposeless events in public space. From 1995 to 1997, Bernadette Corporation worked under the guise of a fashion label, and from 1999 until 2001, self-published an art magazine, *Made in USA*. Bernadette Corporation has also produced films, including *Hell Frozen Over*, 2000, and *Get Rid of Yourself*, 2003, and exhibits regularly at art galleries and museums.